DEATH SUNG
SOFTLY

DEATH SUNG SOFTLY

DAVID ARCHER

USA TODAY BESTSELLING AUTHOR

"...THE NEXT JACK REACHER!"

1

"Sam, look," Kenzie said to him, as he came out of his bedroom. "Mommy made waffles!"

"Waffles?" Sam asked, with a face full of delight. "Oh, wow, I love waffles! Don't you love waffles?" The little girl nodded as he took his usual chair beside her own. "Uh-huh, I love waffles, too, and I love the syrup that goes on 'em, and everything!"

"Yep! Me, too! Syrup and everything!" He watched as Indie, little Mackenzie's mother and his housekeeper and cook, popped two more waffles out of the waffle iron and onto plates. "And here they come!" he said, bouncing up and down on his chair.

Indie laughed at his antics as much as her daughter did, and slid a plate in front of him. She'd poured him a cup of coffee when she'd heard his bathroom toilet flush, so he reached for the butter and syrup that were on the table and began slathering butter into every single hole in Kenzie's waffle, before smothering it in his own favorite original maple syrup. As soon as hers was ready, he turned and started on his own.

"Kenzie, tell Sam thank you," Indie said, and the little girl smiled up at him.

"Thank you, Sam," she said sweetly, and he bowed his head to her.

"You are most welcome, Milady," he said in a fake English accent, and she giggled at him. Indie smiled and patted his arm.

"You're spoiling my kid rotten," she said. "I may have to ask for a raise, so I can afford to pay for her therapy. You gonna be okay with that?"

"Depends," Sam answered. "I think a little spoiling is good for a kid, so the therapy shouldn't be too expensive. Maybe I'll just pay for it myself as a bonus."

They bowed their heads as Kenzie said grace, and then dug in and ate their breakfast. They talked while they ate.

"I've been thinking," Sam said, "and to be perfectly honest, being a PI beats the heck outta being a medically retired cop, so it seems to me that I should put the license to good use and open up shop. How would you feel about being my receptionist and resident computer whiz?"

Indie looked at him. "Let's see, you mean on top of being the housekeeper and chef here at home? Does this job pay better than I'm getting now?"

Sam nodded. "I was thinking I could raise you to three hundred a week, and we'd leave the current room and board as part of it. How would that sound?"

Indie thought it over. "And where would the office be? If it's here at your house, I can handle that, cause it lets me be here for Kenzie."

"Of course it's here," he said, smiling. "You don't think I'm gonna blow money on a separate office, do you? That'd be silly, at least while I'm just starting out. I mean, I've got my pensions, and I checked it out; I don't lose them if I go into business for myself, so anything I make is just extra income. I mean, I know we don't really need it, but it couldn't hurt, right?"

Indie looked thoughtful again. "Where at? The dining room?"

"Nah. I've got a room I use for storage off the garage. It's got a window, so if we clean it up a bit, I was thinking that's where I'd put the office. It gives us a place to talk to clients privately, and it's big enough if we take all the junk out of it. It's even got a separate entrance, on the opposite side of the garage from the main house, so if we put a sign up, we can point right to it. We don't even need to go there except when we're meeting clients."

Indie smiled. "Sounds good to me, Chief," she said. "How would you start?"

"I'll put an ad in the local paper, I guess, and maybe take out a commercial on some of the radio stations. That shouldn't cost too awful much, and if it brings in some business, we're good. Wanna help me set all that up today?"

They finished breakfast and started working on

wording for the newspaper ad. Indie showed Sam how to get a free phone number through Google that he could redirect to his home phone, and then came up with wording that Sam liked. They called it in before noon, but the ad sales person talked him into a display ad, rather than a simple classified, and emailed him a proof so he could see what it would look like. It showed a silhouette of a man who looked a lot like Sherlock Holmes, with the wording:

> *Private Investigator Available. Former police detective now in private practice. Call 303-555-6500 for appointment.*
>
> **Sam Prichard**
> *Private Eye*

Sam thought it was hilarious, but Indie said it would catch attention, so he approved it. The ad was set to begin that evening, and so they called a few local radio stations to get a commercial arranged. Before the day was done, Sam had spent more than a thousand dollars on a month's worth of advertising, and was shaking his head.

Indie sent Sam to buy some office supplies, including some "print your own" business card blanks so she could make some for him with his new phone number on them, and then they spent the afternoon setting up the office, which wasn't hard. Mostly, they just hauled things into the garage and shoved them onto shelves, then cleaned up the mess they'd made. Sam had a desk and some chairs he'd bought from the PD once when they were putting in new office furniture, so he and Indie set them up, added some plants and lamps, and it was done.

Neither of them expected anything to happen for a few days, at least, so they were both surprised when the new number got a call less than an hour after the newspapers hit the stands that night. Indie raised her eyebrows, but it wasn't quite four thirty, so she answered the phone in the living room.

"Sam Prichard, Private Eye," she said. "How can we help you today?"

A man's voice answered hesitantly. "Um—Barry's disappeared, and well, we all thought maybe it was time to get help. The cops don't wanna do anything, so we thought maybe we'd hire somebody."

Indie nodded to Sam that it was a real call. "Okay, can you tell me a bit more about the missing person?"

"Yeah. He's Barry Wallace, the singer, and he hasn't been seen in over a week, now. We're all pretty worried, cause it isn't like him, y'know? I mean, we've had to cancel three gigs this week, and it's really starting to hurt us."

"Okay, then what I need to do is make you an appointment with Mr. Prichard, to come in and talk to him about it. Would tomorrow morning work for you?"

There was a hushed debate on the other end of the line, and then the man came back on. "Um—we can't talk to him tonight? I mean, this is pretty important. If you don't know, Barry's about the hottest thing to hit the Denver rock scene since Kip Winger!"

"Hold on a moment, please," Indie said, muting the phone. She turned to Sam, who was sitting in his recliner. "This is a guy who's looking for a missing rock singer, and he wants to see you tonight, if possible. You up for it?"

Sam shrugged. "Heck, that's why we ran the ad. Tell him to come on over!"

She gave the man the address and said that Sam would see him as soon as he could get there. The guy thanked her profusely, and said he'd be over in fifteen minutes. They set Kenzie up with one of her favorite shows, left the door into the house open so they could hear her if she called them, and went to the office to wait.

A car pulled up less than fifteen minutes later, and Indie showed four people into the office. She hurried to find a couple of extra folding chairs (Sam had some in the garage for when he had friends over, working on their cars) and got them all seated while they made introductions.

The guy who had called was Chris Lancaster, and he was probably in his late forties. He was lead guitarist for the band called Step Back Once, and he introduced the others with him. "This is Stan Bennet, our drummer; Candy McAlester, she plays bass; and that's Janice Peet, she's on keyboards."

Stan was maybe thirty or so, and looked like he'd been through some tough times. His hair was wild and long and seemed to have no idea what it was supposed to do, so it simply stood out in different directions and waved. He was thin and tall, and it seemed he wouldn't look anyone in the eye.

Candy was maybe in her early to mid twenties, chunky and blonde, but Sam could tell from the roots that the blonde came from a bottle. She seemed straight and level headed, and smiled as she was introduced.

Janice, on the other hand, was brunette, thin and nervous, her eyes darting around as if she expected to see a ghost pop up any second. Sam marked her as a tweaker instantly.

Sam shook each hand and said, "Okay, it's good to meet all of you. So, tell me what's going on with this Barry."

"He's dead," Janice said without preamble, but Chris interrupted her before she could go any further.

"We don't know that," he said. "He could just be stoned out of his mind, somewhere, or off on a tear. He's done that before."

"Not lately," Janice went on, "and he hasn't missed coming by to see me every night for weeks, not 'til now." She lowered her eyes, as if nervous about what she was saying. "He—he knows how messed up I get, and he's been helping me cope with things."

Sam squinted at her. "What kind of things?" he asked bluntly.

Janice looked at him for a moment, then lowered her eyes back to the floor. "Barry's like my big brother; it's not like it sounds. He knows I got problems with some stuff, and he's been coming over to make sure I stay clean. He wouldn't miss it if he was alive, so I think he's dead."

Chris and Stan looked at each other, then Chris said, "Jan's been messed up on meth, before, but she's been clean for a few months. Barry got her off it, and she's afraid she won't make it without him. Me and Stan, we think he's fallen off the wagon himself; he used to be a big drinker, and when he'd get really wasted, sometimes he'd take off for weeks."

Sam looked at Candy. "And what do you think?"

She shrugged like it didn't really matter. "No clue," she said, "but I'm new. I've only been in the band a few weeks. I'd love to say he's just off on a bender, but I don't know, man. All I know is I was promised I'd be playing gigs, and without him, we don't play and we don't get paid."

Sam nodded. "Okay, tell me about him."

Chris, who was obviously the spokesman of the group, leaned forward in his chair. "Barry Wallace is probably one of the best singers to ever get close to a microphone. He's got a set of pipes that won't quit, and when he sings, people just stop whatever they're doing and listen, man. I've never seen anything like it, and I've been around the music scene for a long time. His voice isn't like anyone else's, but he's got the kind of draw that Elvis had. People just like to hear him sing, and he puts on a helluva show while he does it. That's what made us so popular, the last few months. We're all good at what we do, but without a singer, we're just another garage band. Barry made us special."

"And when did you last see him?"

Chris rubbed a hand down his right cheek. "We played two weeks ago Friday night, and then he called me on Saturday and said he needed to talk, but he never showed up."

Sam sat and looked at them all for a few moments without saying anything. He had always been a pretty good judge of people, and most of the band seemed okay, but something about Stan seemed odd. He looked at the drummer.

"Stan, what do you think has happened to him?" he asked suddenly, hoping to catch the man off guard and get a reaction that would tell him more about the guy.

Stan looked at him, then, and made eye contact calmly. "I can't even guess, Sir," he said. "He's never done this since I've known him, but I've heard stories about him going off and falling into a bottle. I just don't know what to say; if he's done that, he's probably ruined us all."

Sam grunted, surprised at the clear, articulate answer, but didn't let it distract him.

"Okay, here's the deal. I get a thousand-dollar retainer, and I charge two fifty a day plus any expenses. I can't guarantee results, but I'm good, and I guarantee that you'll get every effort I can put into looking for him. If you hire me, I'm gonna want everything you can give me about him; his Facebook account, email address, cell phone number, friends and family, lovers, favorite party spots, everything you know about him. Still want me to look for him?"

They all looked at one another, and then Chris reached into a pocket and counted off ten one-hundred-dollar bills onto Sam's desk. "How soon can you get started?"

"How soon can you get me all the information you have on him? As far as I'm concerned, I'm on the case as of right now."

All four began to speak, and Sam and Indie both took notes, even though Sam had a recorder going on the desk. They talked for four hours, and gave Sam copies of their two latest CDs so he could hear what they were saying about Barry's voice. By the time they were done, Indie nodded to Sam that she had enough to get started with, so they all shook hands again and the four musicians left.

Sam and Indie went into the living room and found

Kenzie sound asleep, so she carried the little girl up and put her to bed. Sam plugged one of the CDs into his stereo and let it play.

Six AM, it's time to rise and shine
I stretch and wipe my sleep away
Then a thought of you comes to me
Like a summer breeze
And I know that it's gonna be a very good day
And I wish that I could tell you
What a difference you have made
You've rescued me from darkness
And brought me to the light
But I guess I'll have to show you
I don't think I have the words
To make you understand
Just what you're doing right

It's another good day
 For thinkin' about you
Another good day
 For holdin' you so tight
When I wake up every morning, now
 The first thought on my mind
Is it's another good day
 For lovin' you tonight

I spend the hours waiting
For evening time to come
So I can see you smile again
And sometimes I remember
How bad it used to be
Before I opened up and let you in
But lately I've forgotten
Just how I used to feel
When I dreaded waking up
To face the dawn
Life's gotten so much sweeter
And it's all been thanks to you
Baby, can't you see
What your sweet love brought along?

It's another good day
 For thinkin' about you
Another good day
 For holdin' you so tight
When I wake up every morning, now
 The first thought on my mind
Is it's another good day
 For lovin' you tonight

Barry was a very good singer, he thought, and Indie said, "Wow," as she came back into the room.

"The guy really is good," Sam said. "I used to be into rock pretty heavy, and this guy's got more than just talent, he's got that special something they're all looking for. If I'd had that, I'd still be lead singer for Dead On Time, my college band. He's good."

"You said that already," Indie said with a smile. "And I agree, he's really good. I wonder why he'd drop out of sight like this?"

"There are three reasons people disappear," Sam said. "One is what police call 'maliciously missing,' which is when people take off to avoid responsibilities, or to escape situations they consider unbearable, or to gain something; it might be a new lover, a new life or money, like when someone gets a big payday and doesn't want to share it with anyone. Second is when they flee something, like a criminal charge, or if they think someone is out to harm them and run away, or maybe they suffer from a mental illness that leads them to think they have to hide. The third time people disappear is when something from outside their lives is the cause, like if they're abducted or murdered, caught in some sort of accident that leaves them hidden. One of those things applies to almost every possible case of a missing person, as long as there are no witnesses to the disappearance, like in the case of a drowning or a plane crash."

"So you're saying that Barry Wallace either

disappeared deliberately for whatever reason, or someone did something to him, right?"

Sam nodded. "I'm thinking along those lines, yeah. If he got drunk and went on a bender, then he may turn up all on his own, but my gut says this isn't one of those cases. I think Mr. Wallace has fallen victim to foul play, simply because he seems to be a guy who was trying to hold his own life, and other people's lives, together. He wouldn't flake out like this, not without trying to make some provision for the band, especially the girl he was cleaning up."

Indie nodded, thoughtfully. "One of the band, you think?"

"That's definitely where I plan to start. Let's see if you can get into his accounts and find out if any of them might have been hostile to him lately. People are so into email and social media nowadays that they don't even think about sending hateful or threatening messages that way as being something that can lead back to them. And see if you can get anything on his phone records, too."

She smiled. "I'm on it, Chief!"

Sam grimaced. "Indie, please don't call me Chief; I hate that!"

She looked sheepish. "Sorry, Sam," she said.

They moved into the dining room, where Indie kept her computer, and she went online to begin looking into Barry's life. Running him through several databases that compiled information on Americans gave her some insights into his background.

Barry Wallace was not quite thirty, and had a checkered past. He had a number of DUIs on his record, but none in the past three years, and he had been in trouble a few times in his teens, but nothing worse than smoking pot and drinking. He'd grown up right there in Denver, attended high school and college within the metro area, and had a degree in journalism. He'd worked many different jobs, including a couple of stints with newspapers, but mostly he seemed to gravitate toward the music industry.

He'd spent the past two years working as a sound engineer in a small recording studio, and that's how he'd met Chris. They'd become friends, written a few songs together, and when Chris heard Barry sing them for demo tracks, he was blown away. With his encouragement, Barry had agreed to sing lead for the new band, and he'd been building a fan base rapidly. The band was popular in the entire area, playing nightclubs, resorts and even many of the casinos that had opened up around Colorado. Casino gigs were considered a step toward success for a band or performer, and there were rumors of a possible recording contract in the offing.

Barry's parents still lived in Aurora, and he had two sisters who were younger than him. Indie added their names and addresses to the database she was creating, as well as the names of several of his old friends that turned up. After nearly an hour of searching, she had a substantial pile of data, and loaded it all into "Herman."

Herman was a computer program she had written herself that could scan through tons of data and look for common threads, match facts against other facts, and generally find things much faster than human searchers could hope to do. He also found things that humans were likely to overlook, and could compile all of his info into reports that Indie could read. Once he'd done his thing in data mining, she could then tell him to look for what she called "keys," things that people commonly use when creating passwords or security questions, and then he would begin trying to get into email, social media and other online accounts.

She set him up with his instructions and told Sam she was going to bed. He'd been sitting there quietly, watching her as she worked, which was one of his favorite pastimes. Indie was a beautiful young woman, and Sam felt that just looking at her constituted a great way to spend time.

"Alright, Kiddo," he said. "See you in the morning."

2

Morning came, and Sam joined Indie and Kenzie for breakfast, like always, then let Indie show him what Herman had been up to.

"We've gotten into Barry's email and Facebook accounts, and he hasn't been online for at least a week," she said. "The thing is, some of the last emails he sent were all to one person, a guy named Jimmy Smith, who seems to be a talent agent. Check this out, it looks like Barry was being offered a recording contract."

Sam leaned over to read the email she had opened.

Barry, I've talked to Mick at Sony, and they're ready to make this official and get serious, but you've got to get over your stubbornness. They want you, but they don't want your band, and if your guys are any kind of friends, they'll understand. They're a good band for bar and club gigs, but they're just not ready for the big time. You've got to let go of them, and they need to let go of you.

You sign this contract and I can have you opening for Three Days Grace for their entire next tour! That's two hundred dates next year, and you'll be pulling down

10 Gs a show! If you can't see the handwriting on the wall, then I don't know what to tell you.

Talk to the band, and let them know this isn't personal, it's just business. Sony wants you, and if you sign with them, your career is made. Let me know ASAP!

Jimmy

"Did he ever answer?" Sam asked.

Indie shook her head. "Nope. He read it, but never answered it, and it came on the day he disappeared. All the emails from Jimmy before this one, he answered within a few hours."

"Find me this Jimmy Smith, let's see what he's got to say."

"Already did. Here's his number, let me get him on the phone for you." She picked up the phone and dialed. "Hello, is Jimmy in? Yes, my name is Indiana Perkins, and I work for Sam Prichard, a private investigator looking into the disappearance of Barry Wallace. Yes, I'll hold." She handed the phone to Sam, and whispered, "They're getting him."

A moment later, Sam heard, "This is Jimmy, talk to me!"

"Jimmy, this is Sam Prichard. I'm a private investigator looking into the circumstances around the disappearance of Barry Wallace, and I've been told that you were talking to him about a recording contract."

"Damn right, I was," Smith said. "We were supposed

to sign it last week, but I haven't been able to get hold of him. You got any idea where he is?"

"Not yet, no," Sam said. "I was actually hoping that you might have heard from him, and could give me some ideas."

"I ain't heard a peep, but I can tell you what I think. Barry was about to make it big, and I mean big with a capital B-I-G! The only thing holding him back was loyalty to his band, but the label didn't want them, only him. He said at first he wouldn't sign without them, but the last time we talked on the phone, Saturday before last, he said he was gonna cut 'em loose and sign, cause it was just too good a deal to pass up."

"Do you know if he ever talked to them about it? The band is who hired me, and they didn't mention anything about this at all."

"All I know is he said he was gonna tell 'em that night, and I haven't been able to reach him since. To be honest, I'm starting to wonder if he'll ever turn up. There's been stories in the past about somebody about to make it big, but they had to cut someone loose, and then they're never seen again, y'know? This is starting to feel like one of them."

Sam nodded into the phone. "Maybe. Thanks for your help." He hung up without saying anything more.

"He says Barry was going to tell the band the night he disappeared that he was gonna sign without them. If he did, and one of them got mad, we could be looking at a murder."

Indie looked at him for a moment. "Seems odd, if one of them killed him or whatever, that they'd want to hire you to try to find him. I mean, that'd lead right back to them, wouldn't it? I'd think so, anyway."

"People do strange things after they kill someone. Hiring me might make the killer think it makes them look innocent, like the guy who steals something, and then accidentally finds it and returns it when people start looking his way."

She nodded. "Yeah, I guess. Anyway, I got Barry's phone records here; he did call Jimmy Smith's cell number a little while after that email came in, and then he called Chris, the guitar player. That's the last call made from his phone, but there are a lot of calls that came in to it. Several from Jimmy, and four or five from each of the band members, including Chris."

"That call to Chris, that was on Saturday, so that's the call he mentioned. He claims Barry never showed up to talk, and he hasn't seen or heard from him since. If he's telling the truth, then that makes me think Barry talked to one of the others, first. If not, then Chris would be my number one suspect, if I knew Barry was dead."

"Think Chris would call his phone, if he killed him? Trying to look innocent again?"

"Yeah, that would be normal. Wish I could hear if they left voicemails."

Indie grinned. "Give me a minute," she said, and

then went to her room. She returned a few minutes later with a cell phone that wasn't her own. "I got his phone's electronic ID number from his carrier's records. If I can clone this one to it, then maybe we can get into his voicemails and listen to them."

She started punching keys on the phone, and a few minutes later she said, "Bingo! Let's try it." She put it on speaker, punched in a code, and they could hear ringing on the other end.

"Welcome to your voice messages. Please enter your password."

Indie punched in four zeroes, and smiled up at Sam. "I reset it through the carrier's system, so it would let us in this way," she said.

"You have thirty-seven new messages. To listen to new messages, press one." Indie did, and they began to listen to message after message.

Barry, it's Chris. You still comin'?

Barry, this is Jimmy. You get this all worked out? Call me!

Barry, it's Jan, I need you to call me, okay? Or you can come by, if you want. Bye.

Barry, dude, it's Jimmy! Where are you hiding? Call me, we don't wanna blow this!

Hey, Bare, it's Chris. What's the deal, man, it's almost five and we go on at Biggie's at seven. Where you at?

Barry? It's Jan, Barry, where are you? Why haven't you come over? I need you! Please call me!

The rest of the messages were similar, all from Jimmy or the band members wanting to know where he was, and why he wasn't calling them back. There was one message from one of his sisters, all ticked off and asking if he had forgotten his niece's dance program, but that was the only one that was not from the band or the agent.

"Nothing really suspicious, there, other than the fact that he never got these messages. Got anything else at the moment?"

Indie shook her head. "Nope. What's next?"

Sam thought for a moment. "Barry called Chris after he got the email from Jimmy, which lends credibility to Jimmy's statement that Barry was going to tell the band he was taking the contract. On the other hand, neither Chris nor anyone else from the band mentioned it, and they claim they never saw him since the night before. I think it's time to ask Chris point blank what he knew; he seems to be the leader, maybe even the band's manager. I'm gonna pay him an early morning visit and see what I can shake out of him. Call me if you find anything else, okay?"

"You got it," Indie said.

Sam said goodbye to Kenzie and walked out the door to get into his van. They had gotten all the band members' addresses the night before, and he punched

Chris's address into the GPS on his phone as he pulled away. The directions took him into a nice neighborhood in Arvada, and he parked in front of a neat little bungalow, then walked up to the door.

He knocked several times before he heard someone moving around inside, and a moment later the door was opened by Candy, the bass player. She looked at him for a moment, recognition running a little slow, and then smiled.

"Hey," she said, "the PI guy, right?"

Sam grinned. "Right. Is Chris home?"

She nodded and opened the door up wide. "Yeah, c'mon in, I'll get him." He followed her inside and watched her walk down a hallway, suddenly realizing she was wearing nothing but a t-shirt that wasn't quite long enough. He turned and studied the living room until he heard Chris come out of his bedroom.

Chris had also obviously been sleeping, and was pulling a shirt over his head as he came into the room. "Hey," he said, "you find him already?"

Sam shook his head. "No, but I've come across something I hope you can clear up for me. Do you know an agent named Jimmy Smith?"

Chris rolled his eyes. "Jimmy? Heck, yes, Jimmy's always been around, man. He's the guy who always makes lots of promises but unless you kiss his ass, he never delivers. A couple weeks back, he told Barry he could get him on some big label, but he'd have to leave the band, and Barry told him to go suck eggs. Why? He know something about where our boy is?"

Sam studied his face, and saw no sign that Chris was nervous or lying. "No, but he claims that Barry agreed to sign a contract, and was going to tell all of you guys that he was dumping you the night he disappeared. I checked his phone records, and he called you about a minute after the last time he talked to Jimmy. Little while later, you called him back and left a voicemail asking him if he was still coming over. That makes it sound like Jimmy could be telling the truth."

Chris scratched at his beard. "Barry called me that afternoon, said he needed to talk to me and would be over in a half hour, but he never showed. I remember I waited 'til about two, then called him back, but he didn't get back to me. That's it. Jimmy really said that? Cause... that was one thing Barry was like, uber-stubborn about— he flat refused to take the deal unless it was for all of us. He hadn't even mentioned Jimmy in better'n a week, at least. I'd pretty much forgot about him."

Candy came back into the room, then, wearing jeans and a different t-shirt. "What's going on?" she asked.

Chris turned to her. "Remember that agent that was after Barry a while back? He claims Barry was gonna sign and dump us, and he was supposed to tell us that the night he disappeared."

Candy scoffed. "That's bull crap," she said. "Last time he mentioned it to me, he said he wouldn't be any good if he had to work with a band he didn't know, so he told 'em no."

Sam nodded. "Still sounds funny he'd call Jimmy, then call you and say he needed to talk. He didn't say what it was about, nothing at all?"

Chris shook his head. "Nope. Just said he needed to talk, but you gotta understand, that wasn't anything unusual. Barry'd come over to talk about just about anything on his mind. He said I was his sounding board, and he could bounce ideas off me, or just gripe about stuff and let the stress off. He was always callin' and sayin' he needed to talk."

"Okay," Sam said. "I just wanted to clear that up. I'll let you know if I come up with anything else." He turned toward the door, then stopped and looked back at Chris. "What's the band doing while Barry's gone?" he asked.

Chris shrugged his shoulders. "We keep rehearsing, kinda hopin' he'll just show up like nothin' happened. That's what he used to do, y'know, take off on a bender and then walk back in a week or two later like it was just the next day. We're in rehearsal this afternoon, about two if you wanna come by. It's over at Stan's place, we use his garage. A real garage band, that's us." He grinned as he said it.

Sam nodded. "Thanks, I might. I listened to your CD, and it was pretty good. I used to front for a band myself, years ago in high school, then a couple times in college, so I'd enjoy sittin' in on a jam session."

Chris laughed. "Come on, then, man, we'll stick a mic in your hand and let you relive the glory days."

Sam grinned and thanked him, then went back to the van. He sat in it for a few moments, thinking.

Nothing in Chris or Candy's demeanor suggested that they were lying, but it was possible that they had anticipated the question and rehearsed their responses. He was sure they'd tell Stan and Janice about it, but he thought that seeing them in their rehearsal might let him watch their interactions, get an idea whether any of them were nervous about his presence.

He drove back toward the house, but called Indie once he was on the way. "Got anything new?"

"Well, I'm not really sure," she said. "I found the band's fan page on Facebook, and there are some pretty nasty comments there from a guy who claims Barry stole some song lyrics from him, and the songs he's complaining about are a couple of their biggest hits, including *Another Good Day*. He says he wrote them once when he and Barry were jamming together, and Barry just took them and claimed them as his own. The odd thing is, I found this guy's website, and he's a pretty good songwriter; a lot of his stuff does sound like these songs, so it could be true."

"Interesting," Sam said. "Got his name and address?"

"Yep, I knew you'd ask, so here it is. His name is Bill Miller, and he lives at the Grand Crowne Apartments on East Evans Avenue, number four twenty. Doesn't have a job as far as I can tell, and he's on Facebook pretty much all the time."

"Okay," Sam said, "I'm on the way to see him."

Sam didn't need GPS for this one; the Grand Crowne was a hotbed of criminal activity, and he'd been there many times during his ten years as a cop. It took him almost a half hour to get to the place, but he found unit four twenty with no problem, and rang the doorbell.

When the door opened, Sam was surprised to see a very small man; Bill Miller was what used to be called a midget, a very short person who was of normal proportions. Bill was about four-and-a-half feet tall, and if you weren't aware of his age, he would have looked like he might be a ten-year-old boy.

"Yeah?" he said in a high voice, looking annoyed. "Whatever you're sellin', I ain't buyin'!" He started to close the door, but stopped when he saw Sam's ID held in front of his face.

"Mr. Miller, I'm Sam Prichard, private investigator. I'm looking into the disappearance of Barry Wallace, and it's come to my attention that you and he were acquainted, and not on the best of terms?"

Miller stared at the ID for a moment, then looked up at Sam. "You're really a private eye named Sam? Isn't that just a bit cliché?" He shook his head as if he were amazed at the coincidence, then swung the door open. "Come on in," he said. "Barry Wallace is a pain in my ass sometimes, but I don't want anything bad to happen to him. We'll see what I can tell you and if it helps."

Sam followed the little man into the living room of the apartment, and sat in the chair he was offered. "Thanks for giving me a few minutes," he said.

"No worries. You want coffee? I just put some on, and I'm getting me a cup."

"Sure, and thanks."

Miller went into the kitchen and returned a few moments later with a tray. On it were two cups, a carafe, and cream and sugar with spoons. He set it on the coffee table, poured coffee into the cups and said, "I don't mind bringing it, but you can doctor up your own."

Sam grinned, added sugar to his cup and stirred as Miller did the same. He took a sip, and said, "Thanks, this is good." He set the cup down and looked at his host. "Mr. Miller, you claim that Barry Wallace stole some songs from you. Can you tell me the last time you saw or spoke to him?"

"Yeah, no worries," Miller said. "Barry and I haven't been face to face for a couple months or so, but we talk on the phone now and then. He'll call me up when he gets stuck on a line, or can't find a good hook, and we'll brainstorm on it 'til we get it right."

Sam's eyebrows went up. "You mean, still? Even after you guys started fussing over the ones you said he stole?"

Miller laughed. "We're songwriters, man. Every songwriter needs a gimmick to make it in the business, and that's ours. Barry and I go round and round about some lyrics I say he stole, or he says I stole, and people go to hear the songs out of curiosity. They look at our work, then, and see some similarities, and next thing you know I got agents calling who want their artist to record one of my songs, or maybe they think I'm full of it, so they look at Barry's songs and go after one of his. Either way, we both get attention and we both make more money."

"So, it's all a game? Just a marketing gimmick?"

"Yep. Barry and I have been writing songs together since we were kids. The reason we don't hang out is because we gotta keep the image up, the one that says we hate each other. We really don't, and to be honest, most of the songs we each put out are ones we wrote together. We just flip a coin sometimes to see who gets writing credit."

"When was the last time you talked to him?" Sam took another sip of coffee.

Miller leaned back in his chair. "I guess about two weeks ago. He was talking to Jimmy Smith, the so-called talent agent, about a record deal and wanted my opinion on it. Jimmy said he could get him a deal and a tour, but only if he left Step Back Once and let them put a new band behind him. He asked me should he do it, and I said, 'not just no, but *hail* no!' That band has been exactly what Barry needed; Chris Lancaster's one of the best guitarists that ever lived, and he's got a feel for

Barry's voice that's almost eerie. He can make the band sort of mold itself around whatever voice is out front, and that's gold in this business, you know what I mean?"

Sam nodded. "Yeah, I do," he said. "I used to sing in a couple of bands, and one of them had some of that. They made me sound a whole lot better than I really was."

"Right, then you get it. Now, imagine this: you got a guy with golden vocal chords, he can sing in almost any range, carry any kind of tune, and he's got a voice that makes women want him and men want to *be* him! Put that voice in front of a band like that, and you've got the next Bon Jovi or Nickelback or Green Day! You don't just have a band, you've got a band that will put out classic hits for the rest of their lives! Their very first records will still be selling twenty years after they're all dead and gone!"

Sam cocked his head to one side. "Then why on earth would a label want to split them up? That sounds like pure stupidity, to me."

Miller was nodding so hard Sam thought his head would fall off. "It *is* stupidity! The trouble is that a big label can't always see that; they've got some agent shoving an artist at them, and all they know is what they hear. If the agent's talking to a lower-level exec, and he says that it's the artist making the band sound so good, then the exec only wants the singer!"

"But won't they all make more money by keeping a

winning team, the whole band, all together?"

"Sure, they would, but if you got an agent who doesn't like someone in that band, he don't care! He'll get fifteen percent of everything the artist makes, whether the band is there or not. In this case, I know that the agent involved, Jimmy Smith, he flat hates Chris! That's why he wants Barry to dump the band."

"What does Jimmy have against Chris?"

Miller grinned. "This goes back to 2003, okay? Chris was playing for a small band, lead singer was a guy named Stewart something-or-other, I can't remember now. Anyway, Jimmy wanted Chris to come play with a hot Canadian band that already had a record deal, already had a hit record, and was looking for a new lead guitar. He made a lot of promises about making him a superstar, and for once he was probably telling the truth, but Chris wanted to bring Stewart along. Stewart was a good singer; he was not, however, a *great* singer, and the band didn't want him. Chris had to choose between his future and his friend, and he chose Stewart. That band Jimmy wanted to put him in? Three Days Grace! They ended up with Barry Stock, instead, and went on to be one of the biggest rock bands of the century, so far. Platinum, double platinum—Chris could outshine Barry Stock a dozen ways, and they could have been even bigger; if Jimmy had brought them Chris, they would have both made fortunes, but it didn't happen because Chris was too loyal to his friend. Jimmy's an old-school music biz type; he never forgave Chris."

Sam sat there and finished his coffee while he thought over what he'd just learned. If Jimmy felt he had a potential superstar in Barry, and once again lost out over loyalty, would he perhaps resort to violence?

"Tell me something," he said to Miller. "You've known Barry a while; I've got some info that says he tends to get drunk now and then, and just take off, but this guy had a lot going for him right now, so that doesn't make sense to me. What would you guess is going on, here?"

Miller suddenly looked sad. "If Barry Wallace has disappeared, there's a reason, and it's not because he got drunk. My best guess is that someone was really pissed over this deal with Jimmy. Could be Jimmy himself, if Barry turned him down; I know that he has a temper that gets out of hand, now and then. I've heard stories about him making threats if he doesn't get his way, even threats about how he's got mob connections, and being as he's in the music business, that might be true." He paused for a moment, and rubbed the bridge of his nose. "On the other hand, if he really was thinking about taking the deal, it's possible the band might have been mad. Chris is pretty mellow, but that other guy, Stan, he's an oddball. He's got a lot of money, family money, and nobody really knows what to make of him. If Chris made him mad, I don't have a clue how he'd take it. You just don't know about people."

"So you think there may be foul play involved?"

Miller shrugged. "Only other thing I can imagine would make Barry take off is a woman, and last time we talked, he was pretty wrapped up in Janice Peet. I don't know if you know her story, but he got her off the street and off of meth. Barry kept talking like he was in love with her, and I heard that he told her that when she was clean a year, they'd talk about marriage. I don't know if that's really true, mind, but the way he talked about her, I could believe it."

"Would she be violent, if she thought she was losing him?"

Miller laughed again. "Dude, you're talkin' about a tweaker. They can be pretty crazy, especially if they get back on that crap. It's like in the Bible; if you cast out a demon, and then let it back in, it doesn't come alone. It brings all of its friends, and you end up far worse than you were before. If she fell off the wagon, and then he said he was leaving her—even if it was only for a while—it's very possible that she'd be mad enough to chop him into little bits and feed him to the birds!"

"Well," Sam said. "You've definitely given me a lot to think about, and I appreciate it." He rose to his feet. "And thanks for the coffee, too, by the way." The two men shook hands, and Miller got up to walk him to the door.

"For what it's worth," he said, "I really hope Barry turns up. He's the best songwriting partner I've ever had, but besides that, he's a pretty good guy. We have a sort of history together, but I won't go into that. I just have a bad feeling about this, and I don't think we're gonna see him again."

Sam got back into his van and started back to his house. Halfway there, he took out his phone and called his old police partner, Dan Jacobs.

"Well, well, well," Dan said as he answered the call. "How's the big PI doing these days?"

"Working my first official case," Sam replied. "Tell me something; you ever heard of a girl named Janice Peet, that's P-E-E-T? A tweaker?"

"Janice Peet," Dan mused. "Can't say I have. Want me to run the name and see what I find?"

"Yeah, would you please? I'll hold."

"Be right back," Dan said, and the PD hold music started. Sam listened to some bad instrumental versions of old pop songs for a couple of minutes, and then his old friend came back on the line.

"Okay, Janice Peet is twenty-four and has two arrests for using, none for dealing. From what I see, she was probably on it for a long time, and went through rehab about three or four months back. Nothing on her since then."

"Okay, thanks," Sam said. They chatted for a minute about the weather and promised to get together sometime soon, then ended the call.

3

Sam pulled into his driveway a half hour later, and walked inside to find Kenzie asleep on the couch, with Dora the Explorer on the TV. Indie was sitting in his recliner, and he filled her in on all he'd learned.

"So," Indie summarized, "Barry didn't really steal the songs, and Jimmy the agent has a problem with Chris the guitar player, and Janice could be a raging psycho lunatic. Am I close, here?"

"Pretty much on target," Sam said. "The whole thing stinks to high heaven, to be honest, and I'm not far from agreeing with Janice that Barry is probably dead. The only questions are which one of several motives caused which one of several possible suspects to kill him, and where is he now?"

"Okay, then, so next step?"

"I'm gonna go to the band's rehearsal this afternoon, see if I can pick up anything from Janice or Stan. Chris seems to be clean, and Candy's too new to be much of a suspect; I can't see any kind of a motive for her to want him dead, or even out of the picture."

Indie nodded. "Well, I've actually been busy, here, while you were out having gabfests. I did some background checking on all of the band members, and you might find some of it interesting. Come look at what Herman's put together."

Sam followed her into the dining room, and she handed him some printed sheets. Each one had the name of one of the band members at the top, and he scanned over them quickly.

"Stan Bennett," he read from the first one. "Thirty-two years old, ah, he's done a little time, I see. Two years for manslaughter?"

"Yeah," Indie said. "He was driving when his car ran off the road and killed a friend who was riding with him. Since the skid marks said he was doing more than a hundred miles an hour, they cited him for reckless driving, and so he was charged with manslaughter over his buddy's death. He pled guilty and did two years in state prison for it, hasn't been in any trouble since then."

"Mm-hmm. Chris Lancaster has a clean record except for a couple of DUIs a long time ago, but I see he spent a few months in drug rehab five years back."

"Yep. Painkillers, he got hooked on them after an accident where he got rear-ended by a semi-truck. He went in voluntarily, and from what I can tell, he's stayed clean since then."

"Candy McAlester, twenty-two, got a record for, holy

cow, prostitution?"

"Don't get all high and mighty, there, Sam, she had a kid to feed and apparently did what she had to do. I've considered it myself, not long ago; if you remember, I thought you were proposing a little 'take it in trade' thing when you first offered to let me and Kenzie stay here. You'd be surprised what a mother will do to feed her child. Anyway, because she was homeless, she ended up losing the kid to her ex, and only gets to see him on weekends now. I can imagine what that must feel like, and it makes me grateful to you all over again."

"*De nada*," Sam said. "Janice Peet, twenty-four; I had Danny run her through the computer, so I knew about her history with meth, but you've got something here about jail time? Dan didn't find that."

Indie smirked. "Dan doesn't have Herman. It was juvie jail, and after what you just told me, I think she might be a serious suspect. She was convicted of attempted murder at fourteen, a neighbor guy who apparently had been molesting her, and spent the last four years of her childhood behind bars in the Adams Youth Services Center in Brighton. She was released at eighteen, and she's been on drugs off and on ever since. Did rehab a few months ago; I guess that's when Barry started working with her. And incidentally, the guy she tried to kill went to prison, too, eight years for statutory rape."

Sam nodded and flipped to the next page. "And

here's the man of the hour, Barry Wallace. Twenty-seven, no felony record, just some minor mix-ups when he was drinking, apparently. Worked as a delivery driver for pizza for a few years, then started singing with different bands. Looks like he's been with several, before this one."

"Yeah, but is that really strange? I mean, don't singers jump around while they're learning the ropes?"

"Probably. I was never into it that seriously, so I didn't care that much. I just liked to sing." He set the papers on the table and looked at Indie. "You want to come with me to the rehearsal?"

Indie smiled. "Sure. Let me see if Anita can watch Kenzie." She grabbed her phone and called the neighbor lady, whose twins were Kenzie's new playmates. A few minutes later, she woke Kenzie up and fed her lunch, then got her dressed to go down the street and play for the afternoon. When she got back, Sam was ready to go.

"It's a little early," he said, "so I thought I'd offer to buy you lunch. Interested?"

Indie smiled. "You bet! Give me fifteen minutes to get ready?"

Sam took out his phone. "I'm setting my stopwatch—*now!*"

Indie laughed and ran up the stairs, while Sam watched. There was something about the way that girl moved that just tickled him.

When she came back down, her makeup was

perfect, her hair was brushed, and she'd put on a pair of jeans and a nice top that accentuated her shapely figure. Sam cleared his throat and said, "Wow, girl, you clean up pretty nice!"

Indie spun once, to let him look her over completely, and Sam blushed just a bit; the pirouette had shown him just how well those jeans fit, and he had to admit that they fit quite well—everywhere! He kept his thoughts to himself, however, and walked her out to the garage, opening the garage door to get to his Corvette.

"I thought we'd go in style. Besides," he said, "I recall I promised you a ride in it a couple weeks back." Indie giggled as he opened her door for her and let her get in, then closed it. He walked around with his cane, got in and said, "Buckle up," then put the key in the ignition and fired up the big 427. Indie smiled as the car backed out of the garage, and Sam turned it toward downtown.

He took her to a nice restaurant on East 26th Street, and they enjoyed a leisurely lunch of roast beef and potatoes. Sam enjoyed the jealous glances of the executive types that were eating there, watching him with what was undoubtedly the loveliest girl in the place, and let himself think a bit about what it would be like if she was his girl.

They'd pretended she was, once, as part of a plot to keep her safe when he was dealing with some very bad men. He didn't want anyone to know what she was capable of with a computer, so he'd convinced her to pretend she was his girlfriend for a while. He'd even gotten a kiss, once, and admitted to himself more than once that he wished she'd do that again.

Ah, face it, ya big ape, he thought to himself. *Indie's the best girl you've ever known, and little Kenzie is as good a daughter as you could ever hope to have! Why not just admit you're falling for her?*

He shook his head to cancel out that thought, and concentrated on finishing his lunch.

When they were done, he drove them to Stan's address, which turned out to be a pretty nice house on the outskirts of Golden, in a subdivision that allowed some room between the homes. The garage was large and attached, and the door was standing open as Sam pulled the Vette into the driveway.

The loud exhaust caught the attention of the band, and they all came out to see the car. Sam and Indie shook hands all around, and Chris said, "Cool, you brought the wife!"

Sam started to speak, but Indie beat him to it. "Not yet, I'm not," she said with a grin, and Sam stared at her. "I'm just the housekeeper, but he throws in fringe benefits now and then, like getting to come hear you guys play. I hope it's okay?"

"It's fine, Honey," Candy said. "We're musicians, we love an audience! Come on in, we've got some folding chairs in the garage!"

They all went inside, and Sam and Indie got chairs

and parked themselves just inside the door. "Best spot," he said to Indie. "The empty garage acts like a band shell and reflects all the music right to us."

"I take it you've done this before?" she asked.

He grinned. "I was in a garage band before they called them garage bands. Back then, we just called 'em rock groups."

They sat back and Janice came out of the house with bottles of Coke for them, and then the band all took their places. Chris stepped up to the front microphone. "Since Barry's gone AWOL, I'm doing the vocals, just to keep us in practice," he said. "I'm not as good as he is, but I'm what we've got at the moment."

They launched into a rendition of one of their songs, then, and Sam and Indie rocked their chairs and slapped their thighs in time to the music. One song followed another, and Indie commented to Sam that Chris wasn't all that bad, himself.

"Ah," Sam said, "I've heard better, and not just from Barry."

The band took a break after about an hour, and they all sat around talking.

"So," Chris asked, "what do you think? I mean, I know it's not right, with Barry not here, but I think the music is pretty good."

Sam nodded. "It is, it really is. Reminds me of my own days with the band in college. We did a lot of metal, back then, not so much of the pop stuff as you guys are doing, but I always wanted to soften things up a bit."

"Hey, that's right, you used to sing," Chris said. "Wanna hit the mic for a few?"

Sam laughed. "No, thanks, I don't know any of your songs. When I sing nowadays, it's usually the stuff I wrote, so nobody knows if I mess up besides me."

"Do you play? Guitar or anything?"

Sam nodded. "I play a little guitar, yeah. Not as well as you, though, just more of an acoustic style, I guess."

Chris got up and went further back into the garage, and came back with a nice Yamaha acoustic guitar. "Here ya go," he said. "Show us what you got?"

Sam waved it off. "No, no, really," he said, but the band and Indie all joined in to encourage him. He tried to laugh it off, but they wouldn't let it go, so finally he said, "Okay, fine, then, one song."

He took the guitar and moved to sit on a stool near the mic, while Chris plugged a cord into the base of the instrument and turned a couple of dials on the amp.

"All yours," Chris said. "Make it moan, man!"

Sam strummed the guitar's strings a few times, felt out the frets and then began to play softly. "This is something I wrote about ten years ago," he said, and then began to sing softly into the microphone.

She walked along the riverside, the fall leaves blowin' by

And stopped beside a small cascade, a flower caught

her eye

And as the petals fall, she whispers that old rhyme
He loves me, loves me not, which one wins this
time?

And who would believe
That a daisy, after all
Could heal a broken heart
By letting petals fall

She walked along the riverside, and silently she cried
If just one petal had remained, her hopes might not
have died
But as the rhyme went round, those petals blew away
Until the last one softly fell, he loves me not, today

And who would believe
That a daisy, after all
Could heal a broken heart
By letting petals fall—all—all

She walked along the Riverside, her heart lost in
despair
And almost missed the whispered sound of another
lost heart there

She stood beside the willow tree, and watched the lonely man
And listened as he whispered to the daisy in his hand

And who would believe
That a daisy, after all
Could heal a broken heart
By letting petals fall

She walked along the riverside, a flower caught her eye...

The garage went silent as the last note faded away, and Sam looked up to find five people staring at him, their mouths open in utter shock.

"Dude," Chris said, "man, that was freakin' *awesome!*"

Stan was nodding. "I am sayin'," he said. "Man, music lost out when you stopped singing!"

Candy and Janice just started applauding, and a moment later, the rest of them joined in. Sam looked at Indie and saw tears streaking her cheeks.

"Aw, c'mon, it wasn't that good! I haven't even practiced it in years, I'm surprised I got through it!"

"Well, do something else, then," Indie said, and the band all echoed her. "Yeah, man, do another one!" "Encore, encore!"

Sam shook his head. "Okay, fine, one more. Lemme think—okay, I got one."

He struck one note, and then a chord, and a moment later he began to sing.

Life brings with it things that we can never live without

We all need air and water, fire to keep the cold world out

But in my heart I've found a source, to give me all I need

A way to keep me goin' that escapes mortality

I live here in a place that human eyes could never see

A place where every hope I've ever known can be set free

Where my fears can be forgotten, and my dreams can all come true

Cause everything I need I found in you

And I don't need money, when I can spend

Some moments with you, now and then

I don't need water when I'm thirsty

I can drink your beauty in

I don't need fire to keep me warm

When your eyes hold the perfect flame

And I don't need air
 I can just breathe your name

I look into your eyes and see my soul reflected there
 Your smile lights up the path I follow down life's
thoroughfare
 Your strength can keep me standing when I'm weak
enough to fall
 And your love lets me know that I can make it, after
all
 You sing and I hear music other hearts will never
know
 A song of love and wonder that 'til now had gone
untold
 And I'll spend every tomorrow doing all that I can do
 To prove that everything I need, I found in you

And I don't need money, when I can spend
 Some moments with you, now and then
I don't need water when I'm thirsty
 I can drink your beauty in
I don't need fire to keep me warm
 When your eyes hold the perfect flame
And I don't need air
 I can just breathe your name
I don't need fire to keep me warm

When your eyes hold the perfect fla—a—me
And I don't need air
I can just breathe your name...

Once again there was silence, but it lasted for the space of about five seconds before all five of those listening burst into applause. Chris was on his feet, bouncing from one foot to another, and clapping his hands together.

"Oh, man," he said, "dude, that was incredible! I love the lyrics to that song!"

Candy had tears in her eyes. "That," she said, "was about the most incredible love song I have ever heard! I don't know who the lucky girl is that you wrote that for, but she's a fool if she let you get away!"

Indie nodded her head. "Holy cow, Sam, I didn't know you had that kind of romance in you!"

Chris was still talking. "Do you have other songs like that that you've written? Man, I'd love to see us record that, heck, both of 'em! And I wanna see anything else you got! Please?"

Sam was turning red. "Yeah, I've got a few more," he said, "but this is getting way outta hand! I didn't come here to sing, I came to listen."

"He's good," Stan said suddenly. "He's really good. I mean, like he's almost as good as Barry, but in a different way."

"Yeah," Chris said. "I totally agree, man, I totally agree!"

Stan walked up to Sam and looked him in the eye. "Would you fill in 'til Barry comes back? We can teach you our songs, that's no big deal, but we need a lead singer. Chris doesn't have it, and neither do I or the girls. We're all good on harmony and backup, but we need a good lead. If you'd stand in, we could make some of our gigs that are scheduled, and to be perfectly honest, man, we need the money!"

Sam stared at him, as the rest of the band suddenly jumped onto the idea. Even Indie was nodding her head, as Sam was shaking his. "Come on, now, all of you," he said. "I'm no singer, I'm a private eye! I haven't been in front of an audience in better than twelve years!"

"What's that got to do with anything?" Chris asked him. "You've got the voice, you've got a style—man, I'm telling you, this is a great idea. And it might even be the thing that'll get Barry to come in out of the cold! I mean, how would you feel if you were the lead singer of a band, and suddenly you get replaced by an unknown? You'd get mad, right? If he hears about it, maybe he'll come back and we can find out what happened!"

The conversation just went downhill from there, as far as Sam was concerned, but in the end, he agreed. The band would begin teaching him their songs the next day, and he assured them he'd be there at two to start learning.

The thing that finally convinced him to go along with it wasn't any hope that Barry might show up, however; it was Indie's comment that his songs got to her heart and made her feel as if he was actually singing to her. He didn't know what to say to that, because, if he were to be honest with himself, he sort of was. He had specifically chosen those two songs from his personal repertoire because they made him think of her when he let them run through his mind.

4

Sam and Indie made it home about six, after stopping down at the Mitchells' place to pick up Mackenzie. Indie was all excited as she told the little girl that Sam was going to be a singer, and then he had to get out his guitar and sing a song for her, to prove it.

"Never had a child that young call me a fibber, before," he said to Indie, and she laughed.

"My daughter is a lot like her mother," she said. "You tell one of us something, you better be ready to back it up! Why didn't you ever tell me you could sing like that?"

Sam looked at her, letting his head rock around a bit as if confused. "Um, excuse me," he said, "but if I recall correctly, I've known you for about two whole weeks, now. Since I haven't been trying to make time with you, saying, 'Hey, let me serenade you' didn't seem to be too high on my list of priorities. Sorry about that! I'm sure I would have mentioned my music sooner or later, it just hadn't seemed to fit into our conversations so far."

Indie stared at him for a moment, and then stunned

Sam by turning and running up the stairs to her room. He heard the door slam a second later, and then Kenzie came to him.

"What's the matter with Mommy?" she asked, and Sam only shook his head.

"Sweetheart, I wish I knew!"

Upstairs, Indie was lying across her bed, and fighting back the tears that were trying to come.

Just stop it, she thought. *Okay, so he doesn't see me that way, I get it! And like he said, Dummy, you've only known him two weeks; be kinda stupid to be falling in love this fast, wouldn't it? Oh, but why does he have to be such a great guy, then? Why does he have to make me feel like I'm the most beautiful girl in the world when he looks at me? Am I losing it, do I not have what it takes to attract a decent guy anymore?*

She lay there for several minutes, until Kenzie came in and climbed onto the bed beside her. "Mommy, are you okay?" the little girl asked, and Indie dried her eyes as she looked up at her daughter.

"I'm fine, Baby," she said. "I just thought something that made me sad, that's all, but I'm all better now. Let's go make dinner, okay?"

"Okay!" Kenzie said, and took her mother's hand to pull her up off the bed.

When she got downstairs, Sam was sitting in his recliner, but he got up and came into the kitchen as he heard her moving around in there. He sat at the kitchen table and watched as she got out pans, and Kenzie went back to the living room and turned on the TV.

He'd been startled when she took off, and he'd seen the tears trying to come from her eyes just before she did, so he'd sat down and tried to figure out what he had said that hurt her feelings. The trouble with being a cop is that you become accustomed to analyzing motives, and so his thoughts had gone in that direction, trying to fathom what could have motivated her to start to cry simply because he hadn't told her about his music, yet. He'd let the possibilities run through his mind, and finally realized that the only one that made any sense was that she was feeling an attraction to him, just as he was feeling one to her.

The other thing about being a cop is that you become quite confident in your own powers of deduction, so he was pretty sure he'd hit on the answer. The only question remaining was what to do about it, and that's the one he wasn't sure of. He sat and watched her for a moment, until she finally turned to face him.

"Okay," she said, "I owe you an apology. I don't know what hit me, just then, and I shouldn't have done that. I hope it's okay, and you'll forgive me."

"Nope," he said, and her eyes went wide. "It's not okay, not until we talk about it. Come sit down for a minute, Indie."

She stared at him, afraid that she'd messed up somehow and might even lose the home she and Kenzie were becoming so fond of. "Can I get dinner started first? I'm gonna make chili mac, unless you don't want me to?"

"That's fine," he said, "go ahead." He sat and watched as she put water on to boil in one pot, and put two cans of chili into another, turning the heat on low beneath it. When she was done, she came and sat down across from him, watching his face nervously.

"Indie," he said, "there's something I want to tell you, and I hope it's not gonna cause us a problem, cause I really, really like having you and Kenzie here. If what I say upsets you, I hope we can get past it and keep things the way they are, okay?"

Okay, now I'm really nervous, she thought. "Okay— I'll try, anyway."

Sam smiled. "Okay," he said, and then he seemed to be at a loss to say any more. He opened his mouth twice, but nothing came out. It was the third time that was the charm. "Indie, you are a very beautiful girl," he managed to say, "and I want you to know that I notice that. I notice it every single time I look at you, in fact, and I'm sure you've caught me looking at you a lot." He blushed as he said it, and Indie suddenly felt a surge of hope begin to swell up within her. "The thing is, when I offered to let you come stay here, I promised you I wouldn't try anything, that it wasn't like that, you remember?"

She nodded her head, and watched him closely.

Sam cleared his throat. "Okay, well, see, if I'm gonna be completely honest, the more I'm around you, the more I'm feeling—attracted to you. I just adore Kenzie, and I've come to the point that I can't deny what I'm feeling for you, anymore, either. I've been trying not to let it show, because I didn't want you to think anything bad of me, but I can't deny that I think you're a pretty wonderful woman, and sometimes, I think about—us. Being an 'us,' I mean, I think about us being an 'us,' and— I think you think about it sometimes, too." He seemed to be struggling for the words he wanted to say, and paused for a moment to collect his thoughts. "If I'm wrong, I'm about to feel like a real idiot, but if I'm right, then I think we need to be grown ups and talk about it, don't you?"

Indie sat there for a long moment, and it was Sam's turn to be nervous. When she finally opened her mouth to speak, it was very softly.

"Sam, I've been all on my own for a long time, now, just me and Kenzie. I've met a lot of guys, and it's always seemed like all they want is to get close enough to make me want them, and then they're done. I've had my heart broken a lot, y'know? And so has Kenzie, when she gets to liking a guy who seems to like me, and then he's just gone." She looked down at her hands, which were nervously fiddling with the saltshaker, and shoved it away. "When you first made your offer, I thought you were just another guy out to get into my pants, and I was desperate enough I thought about it, just because it would mean Kenzie had a place to stay for a while. But you made it clear, right from the start, that you weren't like that, and even though I didn't believe it at first, I began to after a few days. You could have made a move on me after you bought Kenzie her own furniture, and I'd have felt like I had to go along with it out of gratitude, as much as out of desperation. I would have understood it, even if I didn't really like it, but again, you weren't like that. You were just a great guy helping out a girl who needed it, but then you went even further and gave me a real job—one after another, if you think about it."

She let out a long sigh. "Sam, no one's ever been there for me like you have, and yeah, I know we haven't known each other for long, but the truth is, I think you're the greatest guy on earth. Do I wanna hop into bed with you? I don't have to, but I won't pretend I haven't thought about it, though, and if you tell me you haven't had a fantasy about me, I'll call you a liar. We're a man and a woman living in the same house, we're both feeling a mutual attraction and neither of us has anyone, so of course we're going to have fantasies about each other. That's normal; rushing into something wouldn't be. Do I like you? Oh, yes! Am I thrilled to know you like me? Oh, *hell*, yes!"

She looked up into his eyes. "The question is, what do you want to do about it?"

Sam smiled at her, and she smiled back. "I think," he said, "that we've just taken the first step, don't you?"

Indie smiled back. "Yeah."

"Indie, I would like very much to date you. Would that be something you'd consider at this point?"

Her smile got even wider. "I would love it!" she said.

Sam reached over and took her hand, and she let him hold it. He leaned forward and looked her in the eye. "Is this the part where I get to call you my girlfriend for real?" he whispered, and she burst out laughing.

"Sam," she said, "I can honestly say I thought you'd never ask! Yes, if I can call you my boyfriend!"

Sam reached into his pocket and pulled something out in his closed fist, and held it out to Indie. "When I was in school, if I had a steady girlfriend, I always gave her my class ring. I don't have that anymore, but I wonder if you'd like to have this?" He opened his fist, and there lay his Police Academy ring. "I'm not trying to make this a permanent thing, Indie, I think it's way too early for that, but if I can find a place inside that beautiful heart of yours for now, I'll be a happy man."

Indie reached out and took the ring, slipping it onto her finger, and they both laughed as it spun there. "Yeah, it's a little big," she said, "but it kinda makes me happy that you'd want me to have it."

"Indie," Sam said, "I like you, and I like you a lot. I see how beautiful you are, and I'll admit I like that about you, but that isn't why I like you; and if this turns into more, then it still won't be because you're beautiful on the outside; it'll be because of the woman I see on the inside."

Indie sat there for a moment, and Sam could see tears welling up in her eyes again, but he thought they were okay, this time. She got up and walked around the table, leaned down and kissed him. It wasn't the chaste little kiss she'd given him before, but a truly passionate kiss that said that the future might hold some surprises.

She turned back to her cooking then, and Sam sat there and watched his new girlfriend make dinner.

After they'd eaten, Sam asked Indie to see what she could dig up on Jimmy Smith, the agent. She went to the computer and told Herman what she wanted him to do, and then she and Sam went into the living room and put a movie on the TV. Sam passed up his recliner and sat on one end of the couch, and a moment later, Indie sat down beside him and leaned back against him.

"Well, hi, there," Sam said, smiling down at her.

"Hi," she said. "Is this okay?"

Sam didn't answer, but put an arm around her and pulled her closer. She snuggled in and relaxed, and they watched most of the movie before Kenzie noticed the way they were sitting. When she did, she didn't say a word, but climbed up on Sam's lap and let her head rest against her mother's on his chest. Within minutes, she was fast asleep.

"Want me to take her on upstairs?" Indie asked quietly, but Sam shook his head.

"She's just fine where she is," he said.

When the movie ended, however, Indie said it was time for Kenzie to go to bed, so she took her up and tucked her in. Sam went to the dining room and looked at the computer, but it was just running numbers across the screen. He waited for Indie to come back, and then she punched a few keys, and papers began to spit out of the printer.

"Okay," she said, looking over the printouts. "Jimmy Smith is fifty-two years old, married, with two kids in college, and get this, he's got four felonies on his record. Two for assault, one for fraud, and another for tax fraud. This is not a very good guy, Sam."

"And he's been known to harass people who don't do things his way. The more I hear about this guy, the more suspicious I get. What else you got there?"

"Well, he's been sued repeatedly by people who claim he didn't deliver on his promises, and he's settled out of court with most of them. Paid out a settlement of more than half a million to one band that said he promised them a recording contract that never materialized. He's got some shady deals in his history."

"What about the assaults? How bad were they?"

Indie looked through the papers. "One was against a woman named Samantha Harris, who backed out of signing a contract with a minor record label, and the other was in a bar fight. He broke a beer bottle over some guy's head, then slashed him up with it. According to the victim, Johnny Darnell, Smith was mad because he rejected a musician Smith wanted to put in his band. In both cases, he got probation. The woman was back in 2006, and the bar fight was in 2010, not all that long ago."

"Hmm. Sounds like a guy who might lose it if he doesn't get what he wants, then, doesn't he? I think I'll go see him in the morning, see what kind of reaction I get." He looked at Indie, and smiled. "You done good, there, kid. Now go get you some sleep. We've got a big day tomorrow."

She looked at him and grinned. "A big day?"

"Well, you don't think I'm gonna get up there and sing without my number one fan, do you? We've got rehearsals to go to, and I'm not doing this without you."

Indie inclined her head. "Okay," she said, then stood. She started toward the stairs, but stopped, turned around and came back to him. "Sam," she said, but then she just leaned down and kissed him. "Goodnight, boyfriend," she said, and was gone up the stairs while he watched with a smile.

The following morning, Sam headed off to see Jimmy Smith, who had an office in Denver. He didn't call for an appointment, instead just arriving at the office shortly after it opened at nine. The receptionist looked up as he walked in and asked, "May I help you?"

"Sam Prichard," he said, "private investigator. I'd like to speak with Mr. Smith."

The receptionist frowned. "You're not on my

appointment list, Mr. Prichard, and I'm afraid Mr. Smith doesn't see anybody without one. Can I set one for you? He has an opening next Friday..."

"No, that's okay. You just tell him I'm here, and if he doesn't have time to see me, I'll go on down to the police, and maybe he'll have time to see them."

She looked at him blankly for a moment, then said, "One moment." She picked up a phone and pushed a button. "There's a Mr. Prichard here who would like to see you," she said, "and he said if you're too busy, he can send the police, instead."

Jimmy Smith came out of his office a few seconds later, and Sam was surprised at the sheer size of the man. Where Bill Miller had been a very small fellow, Jimmy Smith was almost a giant; he stood at least six foot six, and was built like a football coach's dream.

"Mr. Prichard," he said with a scowl. "If you'd called ahead, I would have been happy to see you without the theatrics."

"That's okay," Sam said with a smile. "I think theatrics can be fun, now and then. Besides, I didn't want to risk anyone else finding out I was coming, so this was easier."

Smith gave him a menacing look, but Sam kept smiling. "Come on in," Smith said after a moment.

Sam followed him into his office, and sat in the chair in front of the big desk that dominated the room. "I do appreciate you taking the time for me, Mr. Smith, and

I've only got a few questions. Can you tell me about your relationship with Chris Lancaster?"

Smith scrunched his eyes together. "Lancaster? He's a jerk, I can tell you that much. I got him a gig years ago that would have made him rich, and he blew it off like it was nothing. I spent thousands of dollars setting it up, and when it came down to it, he just decided it wasn't good enough for him. The guy who got it has made about two hundred million bucks, while Lancaster's been playing barrooms and dives ever since."

"So you're not fond of him, then?"

"Not really, no."

"Is that why you insisted Barry Wallace had to leave his band behind? To get back at Chris for that incident?"

Smith stared at him for several seconds. "No, of course not. Barry is far too good for Chris and his band, that was all. He needed more professional musicians to back him, and I could make that happen. When he signed with Sony, he'd have had his pick of musicians; they'd have let him have anyone he wanted, no matter who it was or what the cost."

Sam cocked his head. "Then why couldn't he have the ones he already had, the ones you knew he really wanted? You say Sony wanted him so badly they'd have let him choose the band he wanted; why did he have to reject the one he already knew and had chosen? That sounds more like your decision than the label's."

Smith leaned back in his chair. "Look, Mr. Prichard,

with all due respect, I know this business. Barry might have done all right with the band he had, if he'd signed and taken them along, but he could do much, much better with a truly professional band. One of the things my job entails is teaching artists about how the business really works, and Barry was one of those guys. He didn't know what was best for him, but I did."

Sam nodded. "Okay. Now, you say Barry told you he was going to sign, and would tell the band he was gonna leave them, right? Thing is, no one else ever heard that, and apparently he'd been adamant that he never would. The band thought he was done with you two weeks earlier, after he told you he wasn't interested if they didn't go with him."

"That's their story, I'm sure, but then, it would be. They aren't going to admit he was leaving them, even if they had nothing to do with his disappearance, because it would hurt them as a band. If the word got out that someone like Barry thought they weren't good enough, no other serious singer would be interested in fronting them just because they all think they're the best. If this band wasn't good enough for one singer, they aren't good enough for anyone else, either. Simple music marketing."

Sam nodded again. "So the only reason you wanted him to leave the band was so you could help him do better, right?"

"That's exactly right."

Sam smiled. "Okay, got it. Tell me about Samantha Harris."

Smith blinked, and his eyes went dark. "Mr. Prichard, I don't see what ancient history has to do with your current investigation, and I think that this interview is over." He started to rise from his chair, but Sam went on.

"It has to do with the fact that you've got a record of violence whenever an artist doesn't do what you want. According to Ms. Harris, you slashed her hand when she declined a contract you wanted her to sign. I was giving you the chance to tell me your side of it."

Smith sat back down in a huff. "Samantha Harris was a good singer, very good, but she had one flaw; she was nuts about her keyboard man, who stank to high heaven. As a result, she refused to see past her emotions to the fact that the guy was usually stoned out of his mind on coke, and couldn't play 'Chopsticks' without missing notes. When I tried one last time to explain that fact to her, she picked up a vase and threw it at me, but it hit a wall and shattered. A piece of it bounced back and nicked her hand, and she claimed I had hit her with it. If the cops hadn't been idiots, it would have been obvious she was lying, but I ended up having to take a plea bargain for probation because the prosecutor was going to put some of her friends on the stand, people who claimed they were there and saw it, even though they weren't."

Sam nodded. "Uh-huh. And John Darnell? Did he break a beer bottle over his own head?"

Smith was on his feet instantly. "John Darnell attacked me with a knife, and I defended myself! When the cops got there, they took the damned knife and it was never seen again. Once again, his friends all said I had gone after him, and I took another plea to stay out of jail! Now, we are done, Mr. Prichard, finished. Shall I show you out, or can you find your way?" The man was angry and breathing hard.

Sam stood, but he walked toward Smith, not to the door. "Let me tell you something, Mr. Smith. I've got enough information to convince me that you are quite capable of violence if you don't get your way, and that makes me wonder if you know more about Barry's disappearance than you say you do. I'm going to keep digging until I find out what happened to him, and if that leads back to you, then I'm going to make damn sure that I have the most airtight case against you that I can hand to the prosecutor. Now, if you've got nothing to hide, then good; I'll keep looking. But if it comes back to you, then I'm going to hang you as high as I possibly can."

Smith's face had turned bright red, and he was trembling. Through clenched teeth, he said, "Get—out!" and pointed toward the door.

Sam smiled, then walked out of the office. He felt sure that Smith was capable of violence, and didn't believe his stories of innocence for a second, but he wasn't sure that Smith actually had done anything to Barry Wallace. He got to his van and sat in it for a few moments while he thought it through, then called Dan Jacobs.

"Danny, this is a little outside your office, but can you check for any John Doe corpses around the area in the past ten days? Yeah, thanks." He sat and listened to the hold music for a minute.

When Dan came back, he said, "There's two bodies that turned up with no ID, and the coroner is trying to identify them now. One is old, probably been dead six months, but the other is a little fresher and missing some important pieces, like head and hands. White male, thirty-ish, about five nine when he had his head. They're saying he's been dead about ten days."

Sam sighed. "Where'd he turn up?"

"Out on Route Thirty, behind Buckley Air Force Base. Found in a ditch by a jailhouse road cleanup crew two days ago."

"That may be my guy. I'll get with the coroner and see what I can find out. Thanks."

Sam called the coroner's office and spoke with a clerk there, who suggested he come on down and talk to the ME on the case. He started the van and headed downtown, arriving about twenty minutes later.

The ME, a woman named Bertha Ochoa, listened to Sam and asked only one question. "Do you know if Mr.

Wallace had had any surgeries in the past year? This JD has apparently had a bout with a testicular problem, because he's had one of them removed within the last twelve months."

Sam's eyes went wide. "Give me five minutes and I can tell you," he said, then took out his phone. He called Chris Lancaster.

"Chris, it's Sam, and I got an odd question for you. Did Barry have both his balls?"

Chris hesitated, but then said, "No. It was supposed to be a big secret, but he got a cancer down there about nine months ago, and he went to a clinic in Arizona to have it treated. When he got there, they said the only way to stop it was to take one out, so they did." He sighed. "I'm guessing the reason you're asking is cause things aren't looking good?"

"I'm afraid Barry's dead, Chris. I'll tell you guys more this afternoon." He hung up and looked at Bertha. "Looks like we have a winner. Testicular cancer, one removed."

She gave him a sad smile. "Sorry," she said, as Sam rose to leave.

5

Sam, Indie and Kenzie drove up to Stan's place at two on the dot, after a stop at Taco Bell for lunch. Chris had called to say that the band all felt they should go ahead with rehearsals, that Barry wouldn't want them to stop, so they were still on. Sam wasn't sure how well it would go, but he agreed to come.

There were chairs lined up just inside the garage, and they all sat down. Sam started by explaining about his call to Dan, and then described his meeting with the ME, including the way the body had been found and the condition it was in.

"When Chris confirmed that Barry'd had a testicle removed, that clinched it pretty well," he said. "I'm afraid we're now looking at a murder case. If you want me to stay on it, I will, but you only hired me to find out where he was, and I did. Your call."

"You can't quit," Janice said, tears flowing steadily. "You can't. You gotta find out who did this to him."

Sam looked at Chris, who seemed to be the band's manager. Chris looked at each of the others in turn, then looked back at Sam. "I think we all need to know," he said. "We'd like to keep you on it for now, if that's okay. We can afford a few more days, and maybe you'll figure it out."

Sam nodded. "Okay, then. I'm working some leads, and I'll give it my best shot."

"Let's make some music," Stan said. "Barry wouldn't want us to quit over this. Let's make some music."

The rest agreed, even Janice, who couldn't stop crying. The band all took their positions and Chris gave Sam some printed out lyrics to their songs. They chose four songs to work on that day, and then they played them through with Chris singing, so Sam could learn how they went. On the second run-through, Sam stepped up to the mic and sang along with Chris, and on the third he sang alone. By the time five o'clock came around, Sam knew them fairly well, and someone ordered pizza so they could break to eat and then go through them a few more times.

Indie and Kenzie were having a blast. The more Sam sang, the more animated Kenzie became, until finally she was standing in front of him, dancing her little heart out to the beat of the music. Indie laughed happily, and soon she was dancing, as well, holding hands with Kenzie, both of them shaking everything they had. While there were moments of sadness, all of them were enjoying themselves to some degree, and when they finally broke it off at nine, they were all exhausted.

"Same time tomorrow," Chris said as Sam and Indie took a sleeping Kenzie to the van and buckled her into her car seat. Sam smiled and waved, and they headed for home.

"So, how bad was I?" Sam asked.

"You were terrific," Indie said. "I'm blown away, Sam, you're really every bit as good as the guys say you are. I love hearing you sing!"

Sam turned a little pink. "I kinda like singing for you," he said. "I like seeing you smiling at me while I sing, I mean, and Kenzie just tickles me!"

Indie leaned her head back and looked at him, smiling. "So, when am I gonna get to hear more of your songs?"

Sam grinned. "We'll have to see what we can do about that," he said. "Did I ever tell you I cut a few records, years ago? They weren't rock—I was actually in a country music band for a while, and we went into a studio and made an album. I've still got some of the tracks, somewhere."

Indie's eyes were wide open. "And you're gonna find them for me, aren't you?" she asked. "I like country music, too, I'd love to hear them!"

Sam grinned. "I'll see what I can do about that, but not tonight. I think we need to get our little one into bed, and then we can take it easy a bit before we give it up for the night."

Indie was staring at him, and Sam got nervous.

"What? Did I say something wrong?"

She shook her head slowly. "You don't even know what you said, do you? Sam, you just called Kenzie 'our little one,' and that's the first time I've ever heard anyone say those words..." Suddenly she had tears on her cheeks. "That was just so sweet," she whispered.

Sam shrugged. "Well—I guess that's just how I think of her. I mean, I know I'm not her father, but when we're together, I just think of all three of us as being part of something, so that makes her 'ours' in that sense, right? I'm not making any sense, am I?"

She laughed and nodded. "Yes, you are," she said, "you're making perfect sense." She sat and chewed her bottom lip for a moment. "If I tell you something, you promise not to freak out on me?"

Sam grinned and looked at her. "I didn't know people still say 'freak out,' like that," he said, "but I won't. Go ahead."

"Mom was an old hippie, what can I say? Anyway, what I was gonna tell you is, a couple weeks ago, when you left to go to Arkansas after that guy, Kenzie actually asked me if you were going to be her daddy."

Sam turned the van onto his street before he looked at her again. "And what did you say?"

Indie rolled her eyes. "I said, 'Hush, child, we'll see!' and left it at that!" She smiled. "But I can't say I haven't thought about it."

Sam slowed the van to pull into the driveway, and

once he was parked, he said, "So have I. And part of me is scared of the idea, because I've never had kids and I don't know if I'd be good at it, and another part of me is hoping it turns out that way, but it's way too soon to be having conversations this deep, so let's get her inside and into bed."

Indie leaned over and kissed him, then climbed out and opened the side door to get Kenzie. She carried the little sleeper inside while Sam stood there and watched her from the driveway. He looked up at the sky for a moment, and whispered, "If you sent her into my life, then thank you. And please help me make the right choices, where they're concerned."

He went inside and got out two bottles of Coke, then took them into the living room, sat on the couch again and turned on the TV news, just in time to catch the story about the discovery of Barry's body. The reporter was interviewing Barry's sister, Marjorie Newcomb, who was in tears.

"He was the sweetest guy you'd ever want to know," she said, "always had a big, warm heart for everyone. Barry was the kind of man who never met a stranger; to him, everyone was just a friend he didn't know yet. The world will be a much darker place without him in it."

Indie came in as the anchor was wrapping up the story. "That's odd," she said. "Barry's a well-known singer, but they didn't even call any of his band to ask about him, or get their reactions to his death? I'd think that would be just about as important as asking his family."

Sam looked at her. "It would," he said. "Good point, and one worth looking into. For tonight, let's just spend a little time together, okay?"

Indie grinned and came to sit beside him. She accepted her Coke and took a sip, then set it on the coffee table.

"Sam," she said, "sing me a song."

He chuckled. "What, right now? Right here?"

She turned and kissed him, hard, then leaned back and looked him in the eye. "Yes, right now and right here! Come on, sing for me!"

Sam looked into her eyes for a moment, then pulled her down to lean against him. "Okay," he said, "you wanna grab my guitar for me?"

She got up and brought it to him, then sat on the other end of the couch so she could watch him.

"This is one of my country songs," he said, "one we actually recorded. I'll dig that out for you another time, but here goes." He began to play a melody then, and a moment later, he sang:

You all remember the story, you heard a long time ago

The prince was throwin' a party, but Cinderella couldn't go

Then a miracle happened, and she attended after all

And by the time it was over, Cindy was the Queen of the Ball!

But there was more to the story, and if the truth was ever told

You'd learn that hap'ly ever after, turned into somethin' cruel and cold

And if you're wonderin' how I know what I'm talkin' about

I'm the prince who once was charming, 'til Cinderella threw me out!

There ain't no happy endings
There ain't no ever afters
Why don't we stop pretending
With all the lies and laughter?
You know it's only in the moo—oo—vies
Where the boy gets the girl
There ain't no happy endings
Out in the real world!

You know your mama always told you, that love was waitin' at your door

And all you gotta do is find it, and you'll be happy evermore

But you know it's just a fairy tale, like little children love to hear

Let's leave the stories for the children, and cry our lonely, grown-up tears!

There ain't no happy endings
There ain't no ever afters
Why don't we stop pretending
With all the lies and laughter?
You know it's only in the moo—oo—vies
Where the boy gets the girl
There ain't no happy endings
Out in the real world!

There ain't no happy endings
There ain't no ever afters
Why don't we stop pretending
With all the lies and laughter?
You know it's only in the moo—oo—vies
Where the boy gets the girl
There ain't no happy endings
Out in the real world!

Indie sat there in silence as the last vibrations of the guitar faded away. "That was so beautiful," she said, "but so sad."

Sam grinned. "Yeah, I wrote that right after my

girlfriend at the time dumped me, so it was kinda dark, I know." He set the guitar down beside the arm of the couch. "But that's not how I really feel, it was just a way to express what I was feeling at that time. I know that happy endings are possible, Indie; but I also know we have to work to make them happen."

"Yeah," she said, "we do." She slid over closer, leaned her face in and kissed him, and this time, he put his arms around her and held on. They kissed without paying attention to anything else for a long time, and when they finally broke, Sam said, "I think it's bedtime, Babe. Get on upstairs."

Indie smiled. "If I don't go now, I might not go at all." She kissed him once more and then got up and headed for her bedroom. Sam sat where he was for another half hour, just thinking, and then got up and went to bed himself.

Sam was awakened the next morning by his phone ringing, and sleepily grabbed it from his nightstand.

"Hello," he said.

"I hear you wanna know what happened to Barry Wallace," said a woman's voice.

Sam was instantly awake. "Yes," he said, "I most certainly do. Can you tell me?"

"Yeah, but not over the phone. Can you meet me somewhere? Maybe at a restaurant or something, someplace pretty public? This could get me killed, so I'd rather be in a crowd."

"Sure. How about the Cherry Creek mall, the food court? That's always pretty crowded, but we should be able to talk."

"Okay," the woman said, "that'll work. Meet me there in an hour, and I can tell you what you need to know. You'll know me, I'll be wearing a jacket with Barry's band on it."

She hung up before Sam could say another word, so he got up, showered and dressed. It wasn't even seven AM yet, so Indie and Kenzie were still in bed. He wrote a note and left it on the kitchen table, then went out and got onto his motorcycle, fired it up and rode off toward the mall.

The weather was nice, and the ride woke him up quickly. When he got to the mall, he parked as close to the food entrance as he could, pulled his cane from the clips he'd mounted on the bike to hold it, and started walking toward the food court.

There weren't a lot of people there yet, but he spotted a woman in a Step Back Once jacket sitting off by herself near the coffee shop. He walked past her at first and saw that she didn't react, so he got himself a cup of coffee and then went to her table.

"Are you the lady who called me this morning?" he asked, and she looked up at him nervously. "About Barry?"

She nodded, and he sat down. "I'm Samantha Harris," she said. "Barry and I were old friends, and sometimes more than that, if you know what I mean. I can't believe he's dead, but I think I know how he got that way, and Billy Miller said you'd be the guy to call about it."

Sam sipped his coffee, but said nothing. After a moment, she went on. "Barry was dealing with Jimmy Smith, the agent, you knew about that?" Sam nodded. "Well, he came to me last Saturday afternoon, and said Jimmy said he had him a deal with Sony Records, but he had to quit his band if he wanted it. He knew I'd been through that with Jimmy once before, and wanted to talk to me about it, right? So he called me up and said could he come over, and I said it was okay."

She picked up her own coffee and took a big gulp of the steaming liquid. "So he tells me Jimmy's singing the same old tune, and I said he should ditch the bum, not the band. I told him he's one of the best, and if the label really wanted him, they'd have asked to talk to him by now, and he could ask them if he could bring his band along. I mean, sure, they'd probably need a better keyboardist; Janice is good, but she's got problems, y'know. But the rest of them would probably make it fine, right? So we talked for about an hour, and he said he wanted to call Jimmy and tell him the deal was a no-go, but his phone was dead, so I let him use mine. He called and said he wasn't gonna do it, and I could hear Jimmy screaming at him, but Barry finally just laughed and said Jimmy could go flip himself and hung up. A little later, he left, and he's never seen alive again, right?"

Sam leaned forward. "You're saying you were there and actually heard him tell Smith he wouldn't take the contract?"

"Oh, yeah," she said, and then took out her phone. "Here, you can see where he called Jimmy that afternoon from this phone." She showed him the call log, and Smith's number was there. "But that ain't all. Sunday morning, I get a call from a blocked number, and I don't ever answer those, so it went to voicemail, right? Listen to this."

She hit a button on her phone, and it called into her voicemail. She chose "saved messages," and Sam heard:

"Sammie, you should know better than to get in the middle of stuff that isn't your business. I promise you that you're gonna regret sticking your nose into this."

The voice sounded like Jimmy Smith's, and Sam could hear the menace in it.

"Was that it? Has he called you again?" Sam asked.

She shook her head. "No, but then yesterday I got this in the mail." She pulled an envelope from her purse and handed it to him.

The envelope had her address typed on it, with no return address, and it was one of those with the stamp already printed on it. Carefully, Sam used a pen to raise the flap and peer inside. There was what appeared to be a lock of hair in it, but when he looked again, he could see that the hair was still attached to a bit of skin, and there was a mild, foul odor coming from it.

Sam looked up at Samantha. "I'm gonna need to take this for the lab to check out," he said, "and the police are gonna want to talk to you about it, I'm sure."

She shrugged her shoulders. "Yeah, I figured. I just don't want Jimmy finding out about this, cause I know how mean he can be."

Sam looked at her for a moment. "He claims that it was you who threw a vase at him when he was charged with assaulting you, and that you and your friends lied about it."

She stared at him, then lifted her left hand to show the scar of a fairly large cut. "There was no vase thrown," she said. "He grabbed one and smashed it down on my hand in a rage, and my friends and I went running out the door screaming! That lying son of a..."

Sam reached out and touched her hand. "I know," he said, "I know. I figured him out pretty quickly. Let me take this and have it checked out, and I'm sure the police will want to talk to you later today, so stay close, okay? Is the number you called me from your cell phone?"

She nodded. "Yeah. You can reach me on it, or give it to the cops, whatever."

Sam took the envelope with the hair and skin and walked her out to her car, which happened to be in the same area as his bike. He thanked her again, and rode out of the lot, then turned toward the main police station downtown.

Walking into the station felt odd, since he hadn't been there more than a half-dozen times since he was shot a little over a year earlier. He went to the desk and asked for whoever was in charge of the Barry Wallace murder investigation. "I've got some possible evidence," he added.

The desk officer checked on a computer, and said, "That's Karen Parks. Hang on a sec, and she'll be right out."

Sam stood off to one side, and a moment later a heavy woman in a skirt and suit jacket appeared. "Sam?" she asked. "God, it really is you, isn't it? Come on back, and tell me what you've got."

He waited until they were in her cubicle and then handed her the envelope. "This was sent to a woman who contacted me this morning, Samantha Harris. She's also got a voicemail message saved on her phone that may implicate a possible suspect, name of Jimmy Smith."

Karen looked into the envelope and made a face at the odor, then looked back at Sam. "Jimmy Smith, the talent agent? We've had a dozen calls saying he had it in for Wallace, but there's nothing to tie him to anything. We haven't even gone out to talk to him, yet, just because most of the calls seem so hostile; sounds more like they want Smith in trouble than any concern for what really happened to Wallace. You got any reason to think he was involved?"

"Some things seem to indicate it," Sam said. "I know that Smith was trying to get Barry to sign a record deal that required him to leave his band behind, and apparently he didn't want to do that. According to Smith, the day he disappeared he agreed, and said he was going to tell the band that night, but they claim they never saw him. Now Samantha tells me he came to her that afternoon to talk about it, and used her phone to call Smith and tell him it was no deal. Barry left and disappeared, but the next day, a voice that sounds like Smith called her phone and left a warning voicemail, telling her she should stay out of it. This came in the mail to her yesterday, and she said a friend of hers that I'd spoken to said she should call me."

Karen looked into the envelope again. "Hair color's right," she said, "but we'll need DNA to be sure it's his. That'll take weeks." She looked at Sam. "So it's true you went into PI? Is that how you got involved in this?"

"Yep. The band hired me to try to track him down, but now they want me to find his killer. Naturally, I'll share everything, and I'm hoping you'll do the same."

She smiled. "Anything for an old comrade," she said. "I haven't forgotten our time in the juvie division together, or that you saved my bacon there a couple of times."

"Thanks, Karen," Sam said with a smile. "I appreciate it. Here's Samantha's number, and that's her address on the envelope. I suggest you get a copy of that voicemail, have it run through voice analysis. If it's Smith, then he's my favorite for this one, so far."

"If it is, it'll get us enough for a warrant. Whoever sent this to your girl must have Wallace's head in a freezer, somewhere, or did until yesterday. If it was at Smith's house, we'll find at least traces of it."

Sam thanked her again and got up. He made a detour over to Narcotics before he left the building and saw Dan Jacobs at his old desk, so he snuck up on him and put both hands over his eyes.

Dan froze, but then laughed. "Sam, you old son, how are you?" Sam let him go, and he spun around in his chair and stood to wrap his old partner in a hug.

"Oof!" Sam said. "I'm good, or I was 'til you broke me! I figured I've been yakkin' at you on the phone enough; I was here talking to homicide, and wanted to pop in before I left."

"Good thing you did, or I'd have had to come hunting you! You on a murder case?"

"Yeah, as of yesterday. MP I was looking for turned up dead in a ditch, minus hands and head. I just got handed what may be part of his scalp, so I brought it in."

Dan scowled. "I hate murder cases," he said. "I'll stick to drugs and vice."

The two men chatted for a few minutes, and then Sam's phone went off. He looked to see Indie's number, and answered.

"Yeah, Babe," he said without thinking, and Dan's

eyebrows went up a half inch. "Babe?" he mouthed silently, but Sam ignored him.

"Sam, I just got to thinking about some things this morning, and I realized I didn't ever check out that songwriter, Bill Miller. I had Herman do a run on him, and you're not gonna believe what I found!"

Sam grinned. "So, tell me, then, and I'll do my best."

"Bill Miller isn't a William—he's a Wilhelmina!"

6

"Wait a minute," Sam said. "Run that by me again, only in English."

Indie laughed. "Yeah, that's what I said, too. Bill Miller was born Wilhelmina Marie Miller, a *girl*, only in 2003, not long after he got out of high school, he left town for about a year. When he came back, he went by the name Bill, and has been posing as a man ever since. He's only got his mother still living here, no other family, and apparently he's enough of a loner that no one's ever made a fuss about it."

Sam shrugged. "Okay, well, to each his own, I guess..."

"No, wait," Indie said, "there's more! During that time he—she—I dunno, *it* was gone, there was a baby born, and guess who the mother was? Yep, Wilhelmina! Wanna take a wild guess as to who was listed as the father?"

Sam groaned. "Don't tell me," he said.

"Barry Wallace! Is that weird, or what?"

Sam shook his head. "It's pretty weird, all right, but I don't see it having any connection to this case. Or is there something more, still?"

"Just this: the Baby is being raised right here in Denver, by Barry's sister Marjorie. Apparently, since Wilhelmina didn't want it and Barry wasn't stable enough to support it, they signed off to let her adopt the child. That wouldn't mean much on its own, but then Herman found a lawsuit filed about two months ago by Barry, asking to reclaim his daughter, and just to make sure I keep you *totally* confused, according to the lawsuit, Barry was married to none other than Janice Peet! That blew my mind, so we did a search of marriage records, and sure enough, the two of them were married just over two months back in a civil ceremony down in Littleton."

Sam was shaking his head steadily. "Indie, this is wild, but unless you're suggesting his sister killed him, I think it still doesn't fit into the case."

"No, probably not, but I thought it was odd enough that I should tell you right away. By the way, are you gonna be home soon? Kenzie wants you; I told her you were working and she said that's fine, she'll wait, but she really needs to tell you something, and she won't tell me what it is."

That got a chuckle out of him. "Tell her I'll be there within the hour," he said, and then added, "and tell her I love her!"

Indie was silent for a couple of seconds, then said,

"Okay, I'll tell her. Bye!"

Sam said, "Bye," but he heard the line go dead before he got it out. When he put the phone back into his pocket, Dan was staring at him.

"You said, 'Babe,' and then you said, 'Indie.' Is that the girl you had me check out a couple weeks ago?"

Sam nodded. "Yeah, and before you start in, we just got around to realizing we like each other over the past couple days. I woulda told you sooner or later."

Dan grinned. "I'm not complaining! I'm just glad to see you coming back to the world of the living! I didn't think I'd ever see you with a woman again, at least not one you really wanted to hang on to, but this sounds kinda serious. Is it?"

Sam smiled sheepishly. "I don't really know yet, Danny," he said, "but it's definitely looking good so far! She's beautiful, and smart as they come—a lot smarter than me, I can tell you that—and she's got the most adorable little girl you ever laid eyes on, who thinks I should be her daddy."

Dan shook his head, laughing. "Old Buddy, all I can say is I wish you the best! You deserve it, Sam, you really do. But I wanna meet her, and soon!"

Sam grinned. "Well, since that cat is outta the bag, let's go for another one. Come down to Herman's Hideaway this Saturday night, and you can meet her while you watch me make a fool of myself. I'm the new lead singer for Barry Wallace's band, and we're playing there this weekend."

Dan looked shocked. "No! You're lying! Man, you haven't been on stage in how many years? This I gotta see, make sure you get me a seat!" He turned and shouted to the whole room. "Hey, everybody! Sam's gonna be singing at Herman's this Saturday night! Let's all go and make him proud!"

The entire narcotics division exploded into applause, and Sam blushed as he waved to everyone. Several of the people there, detectives and other staff alike, came over to ask if it was true and congratulate him. He didn't get out for another ten minutes, and had to push the bike through back streets to get home as soon as he'd said.

Kenzie, still in her pajamas, was waiting for him at the door when he got off the bike, and opened it for him as he came onto the porch.

"Sam! Sam, guess what!"

"What?" Sam asked, his eyes wide with pretended anticipation. "What is it, Kenzie? What?"

She grabbed his hand and pulled him inside, then rushed him into the kitchen. "We've got a mouse!" she said loudly, then dropped her voice to a whisper. "But don't tell Mommy, she's scared of mouses!"

"We've got a *what?*" Indie shrieked. "Where's a mouse?"

Kenzie showed them both where she insisted she'd seen a mouse under the edge of the kitchen counter, and when Sam got down and looked, he did indeed find a mouse hole.

"Well," he said. "Looks like we need to get something."

Kenzie was nodding her head vigorously, and Indie whispered, "Oh, no," but she was too late. The little girl smiled up at Sam and said, "Yeah, we gotta get a cat!"

Sam's eyes popped wide open, and he looked at Indie. "A cat?" he asked her. "She wants a cat?"

Indie nodded. "Yeah," she said. "I hadn't thought about it to tell you, but when we had our apartment, we got a kitten, and when we lost the place, we lost the cat, too. We couldn't take it with us, so one of our neighbors adopted it. She's asked me a dozen times if we can get another one someday, and all I ever said was, 'Yeah, someday, maybe.' I didn't think she was still thinking about it, though."

Sam grinned. "I may not know a lot about kids, but one thing I'm sure of is that they don't forget much of anything, if it's something they want." He winked at her. "I don't know about a cat, though. I mean, a cat is a pretty important decision. Someone has to make sure to feed a cat, and then there's making sure it gets to play a lot—cats need a lot of playing, you know. I'm not sure I've got time to feed and play with a cat, every day, Honey, do you?"

Indie caught on, and smiled. "No, I don't think I do. If we got a cat, someone would have to do all that, but who would we get to do it, Sam?"

"Me!" Kenzie screamed at the top of her lungs. "Me! I'll feed it, and I'll play with it! Please? Pretty, pretty, pretty, *pretty* please can we get a cat?"

Sam and Indie smiled at each other, and Sam reached down and scooped Kenzie up into his arms. "If we get a cat, Kenzie, do you promise to take care of it and feed it and play with it?"

She nodded her head so fast that Sam almost thought she was going to fall out of his arms, but he held on. "I will, I will, I will!"

He looked at Indie. "Well, it sounds to me like we're off to the animal shelter, then. Why don't you go get ready, Kenzie, while Mommy and I talk for a minute?" He set her down, and she ran up the stairs to change her clothes.

Indie stared at Sam. "Do you even like cats?" she asked.

"We had them when I was a kid," he said, "and I always got along with them. I'd even thought of getting one after I wasn't on the force anymore, but I just hadn't gotten around to it. It was one of those 'maybe I oughta' things that run through your mind, but never seem to materialize, y'know? If you're asking if I'm good with us getting a cat, I am. Are you?"

She rolled her eyes. "I'm a cat lover from way back, Sam, so yeah. But I feel like maybe we're pushing you into things you might not want, and I don't want to do that. I—I like where this seems to be going, and I don't want anything to mess it up."

Sam took her into his arms. "I don't think anything's gonna mess it up, Babe," he said. "If I wasn't such a coward, I'd already be talking about college funds and fixing up the other bedroom and stuff like that, but I don't want to push you, either." He kissed her on the forehead. "I get the feeling you and Kenzie are the best things that ever happened to me, Indie."

Indie rested her head against his chest for a moment, and sighed. "I know I could get used to this. And I understand about being scared, Sam, I'm a little scared, myself. This almost seems too good to be true, and I keep waiting for something to go wrong, or I'm afraid I'll make you mad and you'll toss us out—except I don't think you'd do that, even if I did make you mad." She wrapped her arms tighter around him and squeezed. "You're something, Sam Prichard. Something pretty special. Now where were you four years ago, when I was falling apart?"

Sam was quiet for a moment, but then they heard Kenzie coming back down the stairs, so he leaned back and looked into her eyes. "I've got a feeling I was right on the path that I was supposed to be on, so I'd be here when you needed me most." He kissed her lips quickly, and let go just as Kenzie came running into the room.

"I'm ready!" she announced, and they all headed out to the van. Indie got Kenzie buckled into the car seat, climbed in, and they were off.

The animal shelter was out on West Bayaud Ave, just off of Highway 87, and it took them about a half hour to get there. "An old friend of mine told me a while back," Sam said, "that if I ever needed a pet, I should come here because they don't have all the red tape you have to go through with other places. No waiting periods, in other words; if we find a cat we like, we can take it home today."

"Ah," Indie said. "Sounds like a good idea, then."

They got out of the van and went inside, and only a few moments later they were being shown all of the cats that were available for adoption. They looked at alley cats, tiger stripes, Persians, Siamese and every other kind of cat you could imagine, but Kenzie just kept shaking her head at each one.

"I'll know it when I see it," she said, and Sam and Indie could only smile and follow her. She walked through row after row of cages, and Sam had to lift her up now and then to peer into one that was too high for her to see, but still she shook her head.

Finally, the lady showing them around said, rather testily, that all that were left were some that might need minor medical care, and Sam nodded that they would look at those, too. "Might as well cover all the bases," he said, and they were led into the last room.

Kenzie instantly pointed at one cage that was on top, and said, "That's the one!" Sam lifted her up and she stuck her fingers through the chain link of the cage, and a small cat came to sniff at them. A moment later, it licked her fingers, and Kenzie said again, "This is the one!"

Sam put her down and turned to the lady. "What's the story with this guy?" he asked.

The woman smiled for the first time in twenty minutes. "Actually, that's Samson," she said. "He doesn't actually need any medical care, but he does have a special situation. He had distemper when he was a kitten, and managed to survive it, but it left him with a neurological problem; when he tries to run, his back legs sort of pass his front legs, and he'll end up tumbling head over heels every time. We named him Samson because he was strong enough to overcome the distemper; most cats don't live through it, but he did. If you want to adopt him, you need to know that he may get hurt now and then, from his problems. But there's not a more loving and loyal cat in the world, I can tell you that about him. I'd really love to see him go to a good family like yours."

Sam looked at Indie, and she nodded her head. "Looks like Samson has a new home," he said, "but if I hear one joke about him being 'Sam's-son,' somebody is sleeping in the van!"

Indie laughed. "I hadn't even caught it 'til you said that!" she said. "But don't worry, I won't say a word about it."

"Yeah," Sam said, "I believe that! We'll take him home with us!"

They filled out all the paperwork and Samson got to ride in Kenzie's lap. He didn't seem to mind, and spent a good deal of the time just nuzzling her hands. They stopped by a small pet store and bought a litter box, litter, cat food and a number of toys, as well as a carpet-covered stack of boxes for Samson to climb on and play in, hopefully saving the furniture from his claws.

He was obviously content as they drove the rest of the way home, purring in Kenzie's lap. Indie sat sideways in her seat so she could watch them.

"He's gonna be good for her," Indie said. "I hope we just did the right thing."

Sam looked at her. "If he's good for her, then why would it not be the right thing?"

"Sam, we just went out and got a cat together," she said. "Just like an actual family; what happens if things don't work out between us? Kenzie is feeling happier and more secure than she's ever been. If anything goes wrong and we don't make it work—I'm just worried about her, that's all."

Sam smiled, then reached over and took her hand into his. "One day at a time, okay?" he said, and she smiled back and nodded.

She sighed. "One day at a time. I'll be okay." She pulled his hand up and kissed it.

They got to the house and took Samson inside, and all three laughed as he explored the house. More than once, they got to see his physical problem, as he would get excited and try to run. He'd make it about four strides before his back end passed his front end, and suddenly he was tumbling and rolling. When he stopped, he'd shake his head as if wondering what had just happened, then get up and walk slowly for a bit, but sooner or later, he'd forget and take off running, only to have it happen again.

As noon approached, Indie made them a lunch of tuna salad. Samson got part of Kenzie's sandwich, which she dropped under the table to him, but Sam and Indie pretended not to notice.

Kenzie didn't want to go to rehearsal that afternoon, preferring to stay and play with Samson ("That's my job, remember?"), so Indie stayed home with her as Sam got on the bike and rode off to Stan's house. Sam was glad they stayed home. He had a number of questions to ask the band when he got there, and he wasn't sure how some of them were going to go over.

He parked the bike in the driveway, and walked into the open garage. Only Candy and Janice were there at the moment, and he smiled as he said hello.

"Janice," he said, "could I talk to you privately for a moment?"

Candy got up and said, "Hey, I gotta go to the little girls' room, anyway, and I'll see what the guys are up to. Back in five." She walked into the house, leaving Sam and Janice alone in the garage.

"What's up?" Janice asked.

"Does the band know you and Barry got married?" Sam asked her softly.

Tears instantly fell down her cheeks as she shook her head in the negative. "No. He said we needed to keep it a secret for now. I wanted to tell them all, but he said Chris would get nervous if he knew, so we didn't tell anyone. That's why I said he was like a big brother." She laughed and wiped tears away. "It was so lame, pretending we were just friends, but a lot of people thought I was bad news for him, cause of my problems, y'know? But he loved me, and I loved him, so we went and got married secretly. We were gonna tell them pretty soon, just not yet."

"And you were in favor of the two of you getting his daughter from his sister?"

She looked at him, surprised. "Wow, you found out about that? Yeah, he told me about her, and said if he was married, he could get his sister to let him have her back, but when he told her we'd got hitched, she freaked out and started yelling. Said he'd never be able to support a child, and she wasn't gonna let the kid grow up with a druggie stepmom. It was a big fight, and I felt like it was all my fault, so Barry wanted to take her to court and force it. I guess that's how you found out?"

Sam nodded. "The court filing is public record, so it turned up when I had a computer search done. If you want to keep it all a secret, I'll keep my mouth shut, but that's up to you."

She looked down at the concrete floor. "I was gonna tell all of you today. His funeral is Monday, and there's no way I'd be there and pretend I wasn't his wife, y'know?"

Sam put a hand on her shoulder. "I can understand that. I'll try to help keep everyone calm about it. Do you know the story behind Barry's daughter?"

She shrugged. "With Barry, you only know what he tells you. He said she came from an old girlfriend in his senior year in high school, and his sister adopted her since he wasn't makin' much money, driving pizzas around."

Sam nodded. "Okay," he said. "I'll let you bring it up when you're ready."

Candy and the two men came out a couple of minutes later with cans of pop, and Sam asked them all to sit down while he explained about Samantha Harris and how Barry had gone to talk to her the day he vanished. He told them that Barry had apparently called Jimmy Smith from her phone, saying he would not leave the band, and then told them about the voicemail message that seemed to be from Jimmy, and the envelope and its contents.

Janice started crying at that point, and Sam stopped talking. He looked at her, and she nodded.

"Listen, guys," she said, "there's something I gotta tell you." She went through it all, then, how Barry had told her he loved her, that he wanted to get his daughter

96

back, and that being married would make it more likely his sister would agree, but that they shouldn't tell the band just yet. "I guess it doesn't matter now," she said, "but I just wanted you all to know before the funeral."

Chris and Stan both looked at her, their faces calm. Chris said, "I knew he loved you, that was obvious, and I asked him once if you guys were gonna get married. I wish he'd told me, but it's too late to cry over that now."

Stan nodded. "Yeah, I told him more than once he should keep you," he said. "He never let on, but I'm glad you guys were together before..."

Candy just smiled and took Janice's hand. "You would have made him happy," she said. "I'm glad you got to marry him, even if it was only for a little while."

Sam told the band about the police investigation into Barry's death, and that the lead investigator was looking hard at Jimmy Smith. With the evidence of Samantha's phone message and her statement that Barry did call Jimmy from her phone to decline the contract, it was looking more and more like Jimmy may have killed him.

"Not all the facts are in, yet, though," Sam said, "so we can't jump to any conclusions. Especially in something this serious, we have to be absolutely certain."

"He did it," Chris said. "I know, wait 'til all the evidence is in, but I've been on the receiving end of his temper before, and I'm bettin' on him! I think he did it, just cause Barry wasn't doing what he wanted."

"I think he did it," Stan said. "I've never dealt with

him personally, but I know other people who have, and he's been pretty rough. He's certainly capable of it. If Barry really told him that day that he wasn't gonna sign, then I think Barry got him to meet up or something, and did him in."

Sam nodded. "I tend to agree with you, both of you," he said, "but unless we find some proof, there isn't a lot that can be done about it. What we've got now is only circumstantial evidence, unless they find his prints on the envelope with the hair in it, or they find more evidence when they search his place. If he really did have Barry's head there somewhere, most likely the CSI team will find some trace of it. That's what I'm counting on, physical evidence."

Chris sighed. "Well, the sad part is that Barry's gone. I can't really believe we'll never hear him sing again, but it's true whether I like it or not." He raised his can. "To Barry; Heaven's got a new voice singing up there today, and it's one that will outshine a lot of the angels!"

"To Barry," they all echoed, raising their cans high.

Chris set his can down. "Now, let's make some music. We've got a gig to get ready for, with a brand new lead singer!"

Everyone agreed, even Janice, and they got up and started running through the songs Sam had learned the day before. He had them down pat, so they spent a couple hours on the next four songs, then went on to another four. The show on Saturday night would run four hours, from seven to eleven, with a few breaks interspersed in it, so they had another dozen songs to learn before they were ready.

They worked until after nine, and Chris said he was sure Sam would be more than ready by Saturday night. They had one more day to rehearse, and then would get together Saturday afternoon before the gig to go through the show one more time.

7

Friday morning came to Sam with a surprise, as Samson decided that the old man in the house had slept long enough. He got into Sam's room with some minor help from Kenzie, jumped up on the bed, and started licking Sam's nose with his rough tongue. It only took a few licks before Sam brushed him away and then opened his eyes.

That was Kenzie's cue, and she giggled as she ran in and jumped up onto the bed with the both of them. Sam looked and saw Indie standing in the doorway, a big smile on her face.

"Are you just gonna stand there, or come get in on this?" Sam asked with a grin.

Indie looked shocked for a second, then let out a laugh and ran across the room to jump onto the bed the way Kenzie had done. Sam caught her and pulled her close, then rounded up Kenzie and Samson for a group hug. Both of the girls got kisses, but Samson had to settle for having his head rubbed.

"Mmmm," Indie said, "I could get used to this! Your

bed is comfy!"

"Yeah? You should try it without kids and kitty-cats, it's even better."

Indie looked him in the eye. "Maybe we'll find out, one of these days," she said, and then slid off onto her feet. "But not right now, it's breakfast time. Come on, I've got you steak and eggs!"

"Yeah!" Kenzie said, and grabbed Samson to carry him off to the kitchen. Sam got up and followed, with a quick stop in the bathroom, tossing a t-shirt over the shorts he wore as PJs.

They had breakfast together, and Kenzie made sure that Samson was included by slipping him bits of her own cut-up steak. This time, Indie spoke up.

"Kenzie," she said, "there's a reason why we bought cat food! Stop feeding Samson your breakfast!"

"But he likes it," Kenzie said innocently.

"I know he does, but he's a kitty, not a people, and he's supposed to eat cat food! People food is for people, cat food is for kitties. Okay?"

"Okay," Kenzie said resignedly. "Sorry, Samson, I'll get you your breakfast in a minute." She resumed eating her own.

When breakfast was over, Sam sat at the table and called Karen Parks, the homicide detective.

"Karen, it's Sam," he said when she answered. "Anything new?"

"Actually," she said, "we just got a search warrant for Jimmy Smith's home and offices. I've got two teams going out this morning to hit them both at once. Still don't have anything more, but the hairs you brought in had a bit of scalp still attached, and the blood type matches Wallace. We checked the voicemail message on Ms. Harris's phone, and it was from Smith, so the coincidence of him leaving that message and her getting the envelope in the mail gave us enough to convince the judge we should look closer at him. I'll let you know if we find anything."

"Thanks, Karen, I appreciate it!" He hung up and then called KUSA, the TV station whose news program had first run the announcement of Barry's murder. It took a few minutes, but he finally got to speak to the reporter who'd interviewed Barry's sister.

"I'm just curious," Sam said, "why no one from any news agency has contacted his band about his death."

"That's an easy one," the woman said. "We're a news agency, not a public relations outfit. We were looking for a sympathetic interview, not one that would have people flocking out to see those guys perform. If they want publicity, they can buy ads like everyone else."

"And it never occurred to you that they might have something significant to say? That Barry Wallace's loss will be felt by many more people than just his family?"

"Look, man," she answered, "I just do the news. We did our part, telling people the guy was murdered, and then we get the family to make a statement; that's how it works. If we brought in his band and talked to them, it'd take away from the story by making people think about those poor musicians, boo-hoo, and they'd become stars by playing off the guy's death. That's not news, that's marketing, and it's not what we do."

Sam thought about it, and conceded that she had a point. He thanked her and hung up.

He couldn't think of anything else to do regarding the investigation at the moment, so he sat in his recliner and watched TV with Kenzie for a while, as Indie went about cleaning up the house. He could hear her loading the dishwasher in the kitchen and starting it, and then he heard the vacuum cleaner running in his room. A smile crossed his face as he realized that hearing someone cleaning the house was an awfully comforting set of sounds. It made the house feel a lot more like a home.

Kenzie was engrossed in SpongeBob cartoons, so Sam got up and went to his bedroom door. He stood there for a moment, watching as Indie ran the vac and then started making the bed. She hadn't noticed him standing there, so when she went to the opposite side to straighten the covers, she jumped when she finally did.

"You startled me," she said. "I didn't know you were there."

Sam grinned at her. "I just wanted to watch you being little miss domestic for a minute. Want me to help with that?"

"No," she said as she tucked his pillows into place. "I've got it. I like cleaning this house, and I like looking up and seeing you watching me. Makes me feel like I'm doing this for more than just a job, lately."

"Oh, I see. And does it make you feel like some guy is getting himself an eyeful of your gorgeous little body? Cause I am, you know." He smiled, and got one in return.

"Maybe," she said, "but when I do feel like that, it isn't a bad feeling. Not as long as it's you."

She finished up the bed and came toward him, but he didn't move out of her way. "Indie," he said, "I'm not really in practice at this whole 'family man' thing. If I miss something, or if there's something you want me to do, you'll need to let me know. You won't hurt my feelings, I promise."

She stood on tiptoes to kiss him on the lips. "You're doing an awfully good job so far," she said. "Half the time, I don't think like I used to, y'know, 'me and Kenzie,' but I think about 'me and Kenzie and Sam,' instead. I think about next week, and the first thing I think about is what you want for dinner, rather than what Kenzie and I can hope to afford." She smiled up at him. "I guess what I'm trying to say is, you've got me thinking like a woman, not like a housekeeper, and it feels good to do that again."

He moved and let her out of the room, then followed her as she straightened the dining room. They used it mostly as their computer station, but it still became a mess of piled papers at times, and she liked to keep everything organized. Sam watched as she put each one into a file folder and labeled it properly, once again just enjoying the thought of having her there.

The morning went by, and once she'd finished cleaning up, Indie went to the kitchen and dug out a crock pot Sam had bought back when he was married (and probably hadn't seen since), and set it up to make a roast for dinner. She knew Sam would be at rehearsal until late, so she planned on a late dinner, which allowed plenty of time for the roast to cook.

Thinking of rehearsal reminded her that Sam would be playing his first show the following night, and she called Anita Mitchell to arrange for Kenzie to spend the night there. Kenzie heard her and wanted to know if she could take Samson along, and Anita said that would be fine; they had a cat of their own, so it wouldn't be a problem.

At just before noon, Sam's phone rang.

"Hello?"

"Sam, it's Karen. I thought you'd like to know that a cadaver dog found Barry Wallace's head and hands buried on Jimmy Smith's property. It was in a shallow grave, looks like he was hiding it in a hurry, and we found a spot that scalp piece was cut from. The head looks like it was damn near split in half with an ax, and we're betting that'll be the cause of death. We've taken him into custody, but of course, he's screaming that he was framed."

"Don't they always?" Sam asked. "Thanks for letting me know."

Indie was sitting beside him on the couch, and he turned to her. "That was Karen. They found Barry's head and hands buried in Jimmy Smith's yard. She said it looks like he was trying to just hide them fast and didn't do a very good job of it. One of the sniffer dogs found them. They arrested him for murder."

"Well, at least they caught him, and he didn't get away with it. That means the investigation is over, then?"

"Yep, I'd say so. I'm gonna call Chris and the others, let them know." He dialed Chris's number and it was answered on the second ring. "Chris, it's Sam. They found Barry's head and hands at Jimmy Smith's place, and he's been arrested for the murder. You wanna tell the others, or would you like me to do it?"

Chris sighed into the phone. "We're all here, man," he said. "We got together this morning to go over a new song we want to teach you this afternoon, wanted to have it down before we hit you with it, you know? I'll tell 'em. We'll see you at two, right?"

"I'll be there," Sam said, and ended the call. "The rest are with him, so he's telling them now."

Indie sighed. "I feel sorry for Janice. She's a sweet girl, and the life she's had has been a rough one. This is just one more tragedy for her."

"Sometimes, that's how it goes. No idea why, but some people just have the worst possible luck."

Sam turned the TV to the news while Indie got up to make them some lunch. He watched as the announcer told how Jimmy Smith, the talent agent, had been arrested in connection with the murder of local rock singer Barry Wallace. There was actual footage of the arrest, with Smith being cuffed right in front of his house and shoved into a police car, while shouting that he was innocent and had been framed.

Sam felt a let down settle onto him. He'd been hired to find Barry, which he'd done by helping the ME identify the body, but then he was hired to find Barry's killer. He'd certainly been instrumental in helping to do so, but he felt that the police would have caught Smith even without his help. Surely, Samantha Harris would have gone to the police with what she had, sooner or later, and it still would have led to Smith.

Something was bothering him, though, down deep inside. He went over it all in his mind, thinking through all that had happened, but he couldn't find any other logical explanation than that Smith had killed Barry for not taking the record deal that would have made them both a lot of money.

Indie came in and sat back down with him. "Lunch'll be ready in twenty minutes," she said. "I'm making pizza."

Sam kissed her cheek. "Sounds good, Babe," he

said.

"Mmm, I like when you call me that," Indie said with a grin, so he kissed her again.

"Me, too," he said. "I was just sitting here thinking that we're out of work, with the case closed. We got one call out of that ad the very first night it ran; I'd have thought there would be more interest."

"We've had a few more calls," Indie said, "but they were the usual kind, about tracking somebody's wife or husband, so I said you were busy at the moment. I got all their numbers, if you want to get back to them and take the jobs."

Sam chuckled. "No, that's okay. We don't need the money, I just like being able to work, but I wouldn't want to do that kind of work. You keep telling those kind of callers no."

She smiled and settled herself against him. "So now you're just a rock singer?"

"For now," he said. "I don't know that I really want to do this long term, but it could be fun for a bit."

"And what if some big record label decides you're the next big thing? Would you turn it down?"

Sam thought for a moment, and then nodded his head. "I think I would. I don't think I'm cut out for a life of fame and fortune, Indie. I think I prefer my life pretty much the way it is now, and trying to be some famous rocker would interfere with that. I mean, do you think we'd make it if I was on the road two hundred days a year?"

Indie snuggled in tighter. "I don't want to try. I like this, Sam, I like it a lot; I like being here with you and Kenzie, and I like how much she adores you. I love the way you've taken to her, too. She's needed a man in her life." She turned and looked up at him. "And so have I." She tilted her head back, asking for a kiss, and she got it.

They watched more of the news until the timer went off on the oven, then moved to the kitchen table for lunch. Indie got out the pizza, and Sam cut it up for them, and then they called Kenzie in from where she'd been playing in the back yard with Samson. The fence around the yard was secure enough to keep the cat in, so they didn't mind her taking him out to play.

When lunch was over, Sam got ready to go to rehearsal. Since Kenzie would be spending all Saturday night with the Mitchells, she wanted to stay home with her daughter that night, and Sam kissed them both goodbye as he walked out the door. The sky was overcast, so he decided to take the van, rather than the bike, and drove away after honking the horn at the two of them, standing there on the porch, waving goodbye.

The band was ready when he got there, and by the time six o'clock came around, Sam knew enough of their songs to get through the gig. Chris asked Sam to teach them one of his songs, so they could add it into the show, and he thought about it for a minute.

"Like you've heard, most of my stuff isn't really

rock," he said, "more like country, or country rock. I've got an idea for a pure rock song I want to do, though, and I've got the lyrics and a basic melody all worked out in my head; think you guys could help me get the music done tonight? It—it's sort of a surprise for Indie, so I don't want her to hear it until we're on stage."

They all broke into smiles. "That's awesome, man," Chris said. "Let us hear it."

Sam took a guitar and played the melody as he sang, and by the time he was halfway through the first verse, the band was playing along, feeling their way through the chords and following his lead. They went through the song a couple of times, and then Chris and Stan made a few suggestions that Sam liked, and the final version sounded fantastic. They rehearsed the song several times, and by eight, they had it perfect.

Chris slapped Sam on the back. "Dude," he said, "the girl is gonna love it!"

Sam got home at just before nine, and saw that the house was pretty dark. Indie met him at the door, kissed him a welcome, and then led him into the dining room, where a candlelight dinner was waiting for the two of them.

"Kenzie's asleep," she said. "I let her have her dinner early, so we could have some time to ourselves."

She took the cover off the pot that was sitting in the middle of the table, and began making a plate that she set in front of him. Roast beef with potatoes, onions, and carrots—Sam was amazed, and smiled.

"So, what did I do to deserve all this?" he asked.

She smiled at him. "This is just for being you," she said, and made another plate for herself. She sat down at the place beside him and looked into his eyes. "Sam, you scared me to death when you offered to let us stay here, but then you proved yourself a man of your word over and over. There were a couple of times when I was feeling so lonely and weak that if you'd made a move on me, I probably would have welcomed it, but you never did."

Sam grinned. "Good thing I didn't know that," he said, "or my self-discipline might have slipped!"

She slapped his arm playfully. "No, it wouldn't have. I know you, now, and you'd have told me how tempting it was, but that it wasn't a good idea and sent me up the stairs to bed."

Sam shrugged. "Yeah, I probably would have. I've never been the kind to take advantage of vulnerability, not on purpose."

"And that's why you deserve to be treated like the man you are. I've always wondered what it would be like to be with a man who was really a gentleman, but tough enough to take on the world and win, and now I know, thanks to you. Thank you, Sam."

Sam blushed. "You're welcome, Indie, but don't misunderstand my willingness to do the right thing as lack of desire to do something else. If you think it's been easy not to make a pass, think again. I watch you walk up the stairs, and it's like lighting a fire under a rocket! I do see how beautiful you are, and I see how sexy you are, and I like both. Neither one of us should let our guard down, Babe, not yet. Not 'til you're sure of what you want."

Indie nodded. "I understand," she said, "and I agree. I don't want a relationship based on sex, and I don't think you do either. I want a relationship that's based on two people who actually want to share their lives with each other, and I think we may be headed in the right direction—but we're not there yet. Am I right?"

"I think so. I know I feel something more than just liking you, Indie, and it's happened so fast that it scares me a bit. I want this to grow, but I want it to grow without any pressure from me. Just don't expect me to stop enjoying the view, okay?"

Indie blushed bright red. "Okay, fair enough." She picked up a glass that held cola and raised it in salute. "To whatever the future may hold, and a hope that it finds us together."

"I'll drink to that," Sam said, and clinked his glass to hers. They talked through their dinner, then, and just got to know one another a little better. Indie told Sam about her childhood, being raised by a single mother who always wanted to be a hippie, and Sam shared about his own life, growing up after his father died of a heart attack when he was only fourteen. They talked about their college years, and the dreams they each had held on to, and the ones they'd let go of.

It was a nice evening, and when they finished dinner, they sat in the living room together and watched a movie. It was a romantic comedy of some sort, but Sam couldn't remember what it was about the next morning; he'd been too busy looking into Indie's gorgeous brown eyes.

8

Sam woke up on Saturday morning with a song running through his head, and he had to make himself not sing it as he took a shower; it was the one he'd written over the past few days and finished with the band the night before, the one he wrote specifically for Indie. He didn't want her to have any clue that it was coming, so he forced himself to sing something else while he showered.

When he came out into the kitchen, Kenzie was at the table eating cereal. "Sam! Sam!" she shouted at him. "Mommy's letting me take Samson down to Tracy and Lacey's house, and we're gonna do a sleepover!"

"Yes," Sam said, "I heard about that! You make sure Samson is a good boy down there, okay? Don't let him get into trouble, now."

She smiled up at him. "I won't," she said. "He's a pretty good cat, but sometimes you just gotta keep an eye on him, you know?"

"I know!" Sam said. "He can be a real stinker, sometimes, can't he?"

Indie cracked up laughing, and Sam joined her a moment later. Sam got up and got a bowl of cereal for himself—he loved the kind with the marshmallows in it, and that's what Kenzie was eating—and sat down to eat, while Kenzie finished hers and ran upstairs to start getting dressed and ready for her big adventure.

It was going to be quite a day, Sam thought, with just him and Indie spending it together. They had the final rehearsal in the afternoon, and then the gig that evening, and Sam was as nervous as he could be.

Indie seemed a bit frantic, herself. When Kenzie came down a few minutes later, all ready to go and with a bag packed full of PJs, spare clothes and toys for both her and Samson, Indie was fully ready to take her daughter down the street and have a break from Mommy-hood.

Sam thought they could relax, then, but he was wrong. "I've got to get a bath, and do my hair and makeup, Sam," Indie said. "Since we're gonna be out all day, I gotta get all that done now!"

The band had agreed to meet at Stan's garage at noon, so that they could run through everything a couple more times before they were due to go on stage, and Sam and Indie pulled up in the Vette just a few minutes later. Indie was wearing a dress she'd snuck out and bought the day before, while she and Kenzie were at home alone, and Sam had almost fallen over when he saw it. It was black with gold and silver trim in spots, and went all the way to the floor. It looked good on her, and she knew it; Sam's reaction told her it was definitely the right choice.

Sam was wearing jeans with a gray button-down shirt, and Indie thought he looked hot. Candy and Janice agreed, and Stan ran back into his house to change his own shirt to one that was a little darker gray than Sam's. Chris was wearing a white shirt, and the three of them made a nice contrast.

The girls were wearing jeans and tanks, and both of them were wearing more makeup than they needed. Candy had added in a wig that was a light pink, which Sam thought made her look pretty fake, but he figured it was all part of the band's persona, so he didn't say a word.

They visited for a moment, and encouraged each other, everyone saying it was going to be a great night. Chris told them that the manager of Herman's had called him to ask if they were going to be there, now that the word was out that Barry was dead, and he'd assured the guy that their new singer was every bit as good. Sam didn't think he was, but no one wanted to hear his opinion, so he dropped it.

They started their rehearsal, then, and Indie got to be a one-girl audience. She did her best to make them feel like they were onstage, cheering and shouting and clapping after each and every song, no matter how many times they did it. Sam was having as much fun watching her as he was standing at the microphone.

The afternoon wore on, and the closer it got to time to go, the more excited they all got. At five, Sam suggested they all go and grab a bite to eat, so they climbed into their vehicles and went to a restaurant Chris knew, where he promised they could get the best Italian Beef sandwiches they'd ever eat. Sam said later that he was right, and promised Indie they'd eat there again soon, with Kenzie.

It was showtime.

They parked at Herman's, and Sam and Indie got out of the car. She looked at the building and said, "I've never been here. Is it a nice place?"

Sam shrugged. "I was here a few times, years back. I hear it's getting a little run down, but it's still one of the hot spots for live music in town."

They followed the rest of the band inside, and Sam was introduced to the manager, a guy named Tony. Tony looked him over and grinned.

"Well, you ain't as pretty as Barry, but Chris says you got a sound that's gonna make the crowd happy. That's all I care about. They're getting pretty restless out there, dancing to the jukebox; you guys ready to go on? I know it's a few minutes early, but..."

Chris smiled. "We're ready!" he said. "Give us twenty minutes to get set up, and we'll hit 'em with everything we've got! You're gonna love Sam, I promise! What a sound, man, what a sound!"

Tony grinned. "Just show me, don't tell me! Okay, the stage is yours. Get out there and make 'em dance! The dance floor don't lie; if you're any good, the people will dance, and if you're not, they'll just sit there. Since they drink more when they're dancing, I want to see 'em dance!"

Chris, Stan and the girls began setting up their instruments. Sam asked Chris what he could do to help, and was told to just stay out of the way. "We've been doing this a while, man, no problem. We got it!"

Sam felt a tap on his shoulder and turned to find Dan Jacobs standing there with a dozen of his old friends from the force. He introduced Dan to Indie, and then introduced her to everyone else. The whole crowd decided she was far too good for Sam, and he had to threaten to go and get his gun to make them back off, but it was all in fun and they all knew it. The group of cops found a big table and commandeered it, while Indie found a smaller one closer to the stage and claimed it.

When the stage was ready, Chris told Tony, and a few moments later the lights went down and the jukebox cut off suddenly. Tony's voice came over the sound system.

"Okay, folks, we've all heard the sad news about Barry Wallace, may God rest his soul, but his band is still here, and with a new lead singer! They tell me this guy is every bit as good, but we're gonna let you be the judges, right? Everybody put your hands together for *Step Back Once!*"

Sam took his place at the microphone, and a second later he heard Chris say, "a-one, a-two, a-one, two, three, four..."

The first song was one of their most popular, and Sam let the music come over him the way it used to back in his earlier singing days. His voice seemed to come from somewhere deep inside himself, and he felt the bass drum rumbling through his chest as he began to sing.

At first he was nervous, because the audience simply sat there and watched, and he knew they were making up their minds about whether he was a worthy replacement for Barry, but by the time he was well into the first verse, there were people out on the floor. Within minutes, it was full, and many of them were cheering and applauding already. He heard shouts of, "Hell, yeah!" and "You got it, man!"

The next few songs got similar reactions, and Sam admitted to himself that he was having a blast. His friends from the force were hooting and hollering like wild men and women, and he was laughing in between songs.

When they took their first break after an hour on the stage, he was hot and thirsty, and made his way to the table where Indie was waiting for him, a few feet off to the right of the stage, just outside of the dance floor. He fell into a chair, and she leaned over to kiss him hard, which got a lot of shouts and cheers of its own from the audience.

Sam wasn't much of a drinker, he'd told Indie, so she had a glass of Coke waiting for him, and he downed it in seconds. A barmaid brought another one quickly, as people kept coming over to slap his back and shake his hand, telling him he was awesome or incredible or one of a dozen other words that he was sure weren't true, but felt good to hear anyway. He looked at Indie and grinned.

"I actually agreed to this, didn't I?" he asked, and she laughed and nodded.

"You did, Baby," she said. "Regretting it?"

He rocked his hand from side to side. "Not really regretting it, but boy, am I gonna be tired and sore tomorrow! It's bad enough in rehearsal, but doing this in a live show is a serious workout! I didn't know I could move like that, and my hip is not a bit happy with me for trying!"

"Poor Baby," Indie said. "Maybe if you're good, I'll give you a back rub later. Would that help?"

Sam looked her in the eye, and let a mischievous glint appear in his own. "I don't know about my hip, but the rest of me would love it!"

Indie just looked at him and smiled. "We'll see," she said.

The break was only for ten minutes, and then it was

time to get back on the stage. Sam sang his heart out for another fifty minutes, and the audience danced and cheered and clapped and let him know that, while he wasn't Barry, he was acceptable. The thought crossed his mind that being in the band might not be so bad, after all, and he could still work his PI practice on the side.

When the next break came, it was none too soon for Sam. His hip was screaming, and he reminded himself that he'd known it would happen. He sat down with Indie and guzzled a couple more Cokes while he rested up for the final set. Ten more songs, he told himself, just ten more songs.

He'd planned his song for Indie to start off this third set, and he was getting a little nervous as he got back up to take the microphone again. Chris and the girls gave him the thumbs up, and Stan did a drum riff as he walked up to it once more. Sam stood there for a moment, and then he leaned forward.

"This next song," he said, "is one that I wrote just a couple of days ago, and these guys have been good enough to learn it and let me sing it tonight. That's pretty important to me, see, because I wrote this song for a very special girl, and she's sitting here tonight." He pointed at Indie, and the spotlight hit her. "Indiana Perkins, this song is called 'The Woman Inside,' and I wrote it for you."

The whole place erupted into cheers and applause, as Chris began the riff that would launch the song, and several of them were congratulating her on having a special song all her own. Indie was staring at him, wide-eyed, completely taken unaware by his announcement, and when he began to sing, she felt the tears start to flow despite everything she could do to hold them in. The table full of cops was screaming their support, and Sam put his whole heart into singing the song.

I love the time that we spend together
Feel so lonely when we're far apart
Babe, I'm not tryin' to make you mine forever
Just wanna find a way inside your heart
Now there's some truth in all the things that they say
One look at you is all it ever takes
They take what they want
 And leave your heart to break
And I see those guys
 They follow you around
For the chance to break your heart
 And let you down

Oh, Baby, they just can't see
The woman standing in front of me
All they look at is the part
 That you can't hide
But I'm not after what my eyes behold
I want the part of you that's lonely and cold

And if I fall in love, it's gonna be
With the woman inside!

Wasn't that long ago my heart was breakin'
And nothin' on this earth could take my pain away
Who'd believe you'd come along and save me
A little smile that brightens up my day
I can't see the future
  I take it a day at a time
Just knowin' that you're here
  Keeps me feelin' fine

No, Baby, they just can't see
The woman standing in front of me
All they look at is the part
  That you can't hide
But I'm not after what my eyes behold
I want the part of you that's lonely and cold
And if I fall in love, it's gonna be
  With the woman inside!
Oh, Baby, they just can't see
The woman standing in front of me
All they look at is the part
  That you can't hide
But I'm not after what my eyes behold

I want the part of you that's lonely and cold
And if I fall in love, it's gonna be
With the woman inside!

Indie sat there and stared as the crowd around her went completely wild, screaming and applauding and dancing around as if the music were still going. Sam smiled down at her, and held out a hand, and the spotlight hit her once more.

"That was for you, Baby," he said, and the crowd went crazy again.

Chris hit a lick on his guitar and they launched into the next song in the set, and slowly the place went back to the normal, loud dance club that it was. Sam sang over and over, and the more he sang, the more the crowd loved him, and he knew he'd found something that he wanted to hold on to, at least for a while.

When the final set was over, Sam and the band all sat down together for a few minutes, gathered around Indie's table. Candy patted Indie's hand, and asked, "So, did he get to you?"

Indie laughed. "Oh, yeah, you could say that! It's funny, but all the words in that song were things he's said to me; that it isn't my looks he wants, that we need to take it a day at a time, all of it—and yet, when I heard him sing it, they all took on a whole different meaning, y'know?" She was looking at Sam, and he felt like blushing.

"I know what you mean," Candy said. "You know

what I'd give to have a guy feel like that about me? You are one lucky girl, Indie, and don't you dare let this one get away!"

They packed everything up, and Chris went to get paid. When he came out, he handed Sam a stack of bills.

"What's this?" Sam asked.

"Your cut, man. Everybody gets fifteen percent of the gig, and the rest goes into the operating fund. We got two grand for the gig, so there's three hundred bucks there for you."

Sam looked at the money in his hand. "I almost feel bad, taking this," he said. "Maybe—maybe this should go into a memorial for Barry, or something."

Chris shook his head. "No, man, you stepped up and did the job, so you get the pay. Trust me when I say Barry would want it that way. He was as fair and honest as they come, he'd want it this way, I promise."

Sam nodded and slipped the money into his pocket, and then it was time to go. He walked Indie out to the Vette, limping all the way and leaning heavily on his cane, but still insisted on opening her door for her, and closing it when he was in. He went around to the driver's door and got behind the wheel, then looked over at her.

"Well," he said, "how did I really do?"

Indie smiled at him, and then leaned over and kissed him with everything she had. Sam put his arms around her and pulled her close, and the kiss got even hotter, until he finally said, "Whoa, we gotta stop this!"

"Why?" Indie whispered into his ear.

"Because this is a Corvette, and there isn't enough room in this car for what's about to happen if you don't stop, right now! I've been a gentleman, but a guy can only take so much, Baby, and you're pushing all my buttons!"

Indie slid back into her own seat and smiled at him. "Then I suggest you get us home," she said in a sultry voice, "so I can show you just how much you really got to me tonight!"

Sam fired up the Vette and left rubber on the parking lot pavement. He drove as calmly as he could, but Indie was caressing his arm and running her hand on his right leg, and he was doing all he could to force himself to remember the rules of the road.

9

Sam's phone woke him the next morning, and he woke groggily to reach for it, but couldn't move his arm. A second later he was wide awake, as he realized that the reason it wouldn't move was because Indie was lying on it. Instantly, he remembered the night before, and exactly how she'd shown him how he'd gotten to her with his song, and the smile that spread across his face was a mile wide.

The phone was still ringing, though, so he reached with his other arm behind his head to get it.

"Hello?" he said, and then a recording began to play.

"Hello. This call is from..." A new voice said, "Jimmy Smith," followed by the original voice saying, "...who is an inmate at the county jail. To accept the call, dial five. To decline the call and block all future calls from this inmate, dial nine."

Sam looked at the phone and thought for a second, then pressed the number five. A second later, he heard sounds in the background on the other end.

"Hello?" he said again.

"Hey, man, thanks for taking the call. Listen, I was wondering if you would come down and see me."

Sam shook his head. "Why is that, Jimmy? I mean, I didn't put you there, the cops did."

Smith laughed ironically. "Yeah, I know," he said, "but here's the thing. I didn't do it. I did not kill Barry Wallace, and someone is going to great lengths to make it look like I did. If I don't get some serious help real soon, Mr. Prichard, I'm gonna find myself standing trial for a murder I didn't commit, and the way it looks, even I would convict me! I need help, and you're the only guy I trust, right at the moment."

"Jimmy, why would you trust me? From what I've been told, you seem to be the only viable suspect in this case. Why do you think I can help you?"

"Look, Mr. Prichard, the cops aren't even trying to look for anyone else in this case, they think they got the right guy, and with the evidence stacking up the way it does, I can't blame them. That doesn't change the fact that I did not do it, though, so I need someone who knows how to investigate properly, and you seem to be about the only PI in the whole damn state worth his salt. I need someone with your experience and skills, and you're the only one who really wants to see the truth in this case. Now, I can pay you whatever you want, and I will; I just need your help."

Sam thought for a long moment, and the first thing that crossed his mind was that he'd had some kind of misgivings about the way the case was solved so easily.

"I'll come down," he said. "What time is visiting hours?"

"They start at noon, but I asked the head jailer, and he said if I hire a PI or a lawyer, they can come anytime and we can go into a meeting room and talk privately. I'll be ready anytime, just come as soon as you can, okay?"

Sam sighed. "I'll be there in a couple of hours," he said.

Smith let out a sigh of his own. "Thanks, Mr. Prichard, I really appreciate it. I'll talk to you then."

Sam put down the phone, and noticed that Indie was awake and looking at him. "Jimmy Smith?" she asked.

"Yep. He says he didn't do it, and wants to hire me to try to prove it."

"You think there's any chance he's telling the truth?"

Sam nodded. "Strange as it may seem, Babe, I think there might be. Something about the way the case ended has been bothering me, like there's something I've overlooked. I think I want to hear what he's got to say."

"I heard you say you'd be there in two hours. How long does it take you to get there?"

"Half hour or so."

"Good," she said, "cause I'm not done with you yet." She rolled over on top of him, and he stopped thinking about Jimmy Smith.

An hour later, he got up and showered while Indie

went back to sleep for a while, then slipped into his clothes and out the front door. He drove the van downtown to the jail and told the jailer he was there as a PI to see Jimmy Smith. A few minutes later, another jailer came to escort him to an interview room normally used by police and lawyers.

"You sit here," the jailer said, indicating one of a pair of chairs on one side of a table. "Smith will sit across from you. If he gets violent or anything, just yell, and one of us will be right outside. I don't know if you've seen him, but he's a big son of a bitch!"

"I know him," Sam said, and the jailer nodded and left. A moment later, he returned with Smith and told him to sit in his chair and not to get out of it for any reason.

"No problem," Smith said, and the jailer left them alone.

"Mr. Prichard," he began, but Sam held up a hand to stop him.

"Just Sam," he said, and Smith nodded.

"Thanks for coming, Sam. I know it must have been a hard decision, especially after the last time we met. I wasn't very polite, and I apologize for it."

Sam shrugged. "I was pretty rude, myself, that day. Let's forget that and get on to this. To be honest, I wasn't a hundred percent convinced you were guilty, and I guess I'm still not. Tell me your side of it."

"That's part of the problem," Smith said, "I don't

even have a side to tell. I have no idea how Barry died, and no clue how his head ended up on my property. The place where they found it, that spot is back by the road behind my place, and if you ask me, anyone could have driven up there in the middle of the night, got out and buried that stuff, and been gone before anyone noticed. I sure didn't hear anything."

Sam sat there and looked at him for a minute. "I've talked to someone who says Barry called you from her phone and said he wasn't interested in your record deal, a few hours after you say he told you he'd sign and leave the band."

Smith nodded. "I heard. Samantha Harris. I got a call from her that day, but it wasn't from Barry. She called me and said Barry asked her to call and say he wasn't interested. I said that was BS, but she insisted it was true, so I started trying to call Barry and he never answered. I figured she talked him out of it, and that he just wasn't answering for me, and that's when I called her and left the message they're using against me. I was trying to tell her to butt out, was all, cause I figured she was talking him into ignoring me."

Sam thought it through. He'd seen the call to Smith's phone on Samantha's, but there was no way to know who had placed it, of course. Smith could be telling the truth.

"What did the cops say when you told them this?"

Smith snorted. "I asked them to put me on a polygraph, and they said it wasn't worth their time and effort. They basically said they've got me, so they're not gonna look for anyone else. That's why I thought to call you, Sam."

"So who do you think is framing you? Samantha Harris?"

"Nah, she's not this smart," Smith said. "But I can guarantee you she knows who's doing it, and is working right along with 'em! Otherwise, she'd never have thought to say Barry called me that day from her phone. She'd have tried to pretend she never talked to me at all."

"Then who else could it be? It'd have to be someone who hated Barry enough to kill him, and hated you enough to want you to go down for it. Any ideas?"

Smith nodded. "Two possibilities," he said. "One would be Chris Lancaster; we've had a problem since I tried to get him in with that big band, and he's run his mouth several times about wanting to see me get what he says I deserve, and if Barry did say he was leaving the band, he'd have been hot enough to flip his lid. He'd be the first one I'd look at."

"And the second?"

"Barry's sister, Marjorie. Back when I started working with Chris, Barry told me about how his sister was raising his kid, and he was trying to make enough money he could get her back. I thought if I could help him out with that, then he'd sign the contract and I'd be home free and making the big money, so I went to talk to her. She and her husband went absolutely nuts on me; she even pulled a gun and threatened to shoot me if I ever talked to her again! She said she'd see Barry rot in hell before she ever let him have his daughter back, and that if I didn't stay out of it, she'd send me there right along with him. She's a nutcase, and I guarantee you she'd be capable of killing her own brother!"

Sam sat there for another long moment, just considering what Smith had said. If he was telling the truth, and there was no reason to doubt him at the moment, then it was very possible that he was innocent. Sam wasn't convinced that Chris was a killer, but the sister was an unknown quantity.

"Let's assume for the moment that I believe you're innocent. There still are no guarantees that I can prove that. You do understand that, right?"

Smith nodded. "I know," he said, "but you're the only hope I've got. I'll pay you fifty thousand to get your ass out there and try to find the real killer, Sam. If you manage it, I'll give you another fifty on top of that. Fair enough?"

Sam nodded. "Fair enough," he said. "How do I get the money? They let you have a check book in here?"

"No, but I talked this over with my wife Sheila last night, and she said to call you. I'll give you her number, and she'll give it to you in cash today."

Sam's eyebrows went up. "You keep that kind of money around in cash?"

"Hey, sometimes cash is what makes the big deals

happen! I keep better than half a million in cash there in a safe, just in case I need it. Just call her and she'll let you have it. And Sam? Thank you, and I mean that from the bottom of my heart."

"If you really are innocent," Sam said, "then I'm gonna do my best to prove it. If you're not, and you're playing me, then I'm gonna take your money and enjoy the heck out of it while you rot in prison, understood?"

Smith stood up and extended a hand. "Perfectly," he said, "and I'd feel exactly the same way if I was you!"

Sam shook his hand, and then knocked to let the jailer know he was done. The same one came and escorted Smith back to his cell, while another walked Sam out.

When he got outside, he dialed the number Smith had given him, and a woman answered.

"Mrs. Smith, this is Sam Prichard," he said, and she started talking and crying all at once.

"Oh, thank God, Mr. Prichard, thank God you called! You talked to Jimmy already?"

"Yes, he told me—"

"To call me, yes," she said. "I've got the money for you now, fifty thousand dollars in cash. Can you come by for it, or do you want me to bring it to you somewhere?"

"I can come by. I can be there about thirty minutes, is that alright?"

"Yes, yes, I'll be here! And thank you, thank you so much for being willing to help!"

Sam hung up and got into the van to drive to the Smith place, a fairly large mansion on the edge of the city. He got there just when he'd said he would, and Mrs. Smith answered the doorbell instantly. She was a ravishingly beautiful woman, a few years younger than her husband, but obviously in great shape. She invited him in, and he stepped into a grand foyer, then followed her into her kitchen.

She picked up a small cloth bag, the kind used by upscale stores, and handed it to him. Sam glanced inside and saw several stacks of bills with paper bank wrappers still on them. Each was marked $1000, and he estimated that there were probably fifty of them, as promised. He didn't bother to count it.

"Mr. Prichard," she said, "I do thank you for helping us. Jimmy isn't nearly as bad a man as some people think, and this is very hard on our whole family. I know he didn't do this, Mr. Prichard, I *know* he didn't do it. I even told the police, how he was with me the whole day that Barry disappeared; I was here when Barry called him, and when that woman called him, too. I know for sure that he's innocent, but the police think I'm just lying to try to protect him, and I guess I can see why they'd think a wife would do that, but I'm telling the truth!"

Sam looked at her for a moment, and then asked a question. "Mrs. Smith, would you have any ideas who might want to frame your husband for murder? Does anyone come to mind when you think about it?"

She looked him in the eye for a long moment, and then asked one of her own. "Mr. Prichard, is a private investigator like a lawyer? Do you keep confidential what your clients tell you?"

"We're not protected by the law on such matters, Mrs. Smith, but I can give you my word on it. Anything you tell me will stay between us."

Mrs. Smith stood there for a few seconds, then said, "Mr. Prichard, my husband is a good provider and a wonderful father, but he's also a man, and sometimes he strays. This Samantha Harris was one of those he has strayed with in the past, and the truth about the time he supposedly assaulted her is that they got into a fight because he would not leave me and marry her. That's what caused her to back out of the contract he was working on for her, and that led to the big fight. If you ask me, she's had it in for him ever since, and since she's the one who supposedly came up with all this evidence..."

"Then you think she's behind it? I asked Jimmy about her, and he said she isn't smart enough to do this on her own."

Mrs. Smith smiled, but it was a bitter smile. "My husband has a low opinion of the female intelligence, I'm afraid. Is she smart enough? Oh, yes, she's very intelligent, and very devious! I think she's quite capable of doing this, and I know she's had some sort of relationship with Barry that was pretty rocky, too. I'm not sure what it was all about, but there were times when she loved him, and others when she hated his guts!"

Sam let her words digest for a moment. "I'll do what I can, Mrs. Smith. Meanwhile, if you have any ideas or need anything from me, here's my number." He handed her one of the homemade business cards. "Just call me." He started to turn and leave, but she caught his arm.

"Mr. Prichard, please find out who did this," she said. "And if what I've given you isn't enough, or if there's —anything else you might want, as an incentive—please let me know. I'd give you anything to help my husband, because no one else will."

Sam smiled, but assured her the money was more than enough, and he thought he detected a hint of disappointment in her face as he turned away. He'd known instantly what she was offering, but he wasn't interested, especially now that he had the woman he truly wanted waiting for him at home. This was one conversation he wouldn't be telling her about; Indie might be small, but he'd bet she could take Mrs. Smith in a fair fight.

He got back into his van and glanced into the bag full of money again. What was it about people nowadays, always giving him cash? Didn't anyone know how to write a check anymore?

He called Indie and told her that he'd accepted the

case, and that he'd picked up the money, but wanted to go and try to see Samantha Harris, to see if he could rattle her at all. She went to the computer and found the woman's address in a matter of seconds, and he was on the way.

Samantha Harris lived in Arvada, so it was about a forty-minute drive from where he was to her place. He pulled up and parked on the street in front of her townhouse, and walked up to ring her bell. She answered almost immediately, and seemed very surprised to see him standing there.

"Ms. Harris, I was wondering if I could ask you a few more questions," he said, and she opened the door wide so he could enter.

"I thought everything was over, now that Jimmy's been arrested," she said.

"Well, I'm just trying to clear up a few details," Sam said, "and I was hoping you could help."

She shrugged. "Sure, if I can. Have a seat." She pointed to her couch and he sat.

"Okay, now, according to Jimmy, it wasn't Barry who called him from your phone that day, it was you. He claims you said that Barry asked you to call and tell him he wasn't going to sign the contract, and that that was the real reason for the voicemail message he left you."

She laughed. "Oh, good grief," she said, "he actually said that? What a liar! No, like I said, Barry's phone was dead and he used mine to tell Jimmy to forget it. That's the honest truth."

Sam couldn't tell if she was being honest or not, for sure. She seemed relaxed enough, but something was off. "Okay, thanks. Now, can you tell me about your affair with Jimmy? That was back before your hand got hurt, right?"

Her eyes went dark, suddenly. "Yeah, we had a fling once," she said through clinched teeth, "years ago. He kept telling me I was the most beautiful woman he'd ever seen, and how he wished I was his kids' mother, all the crap married men say when they want to get into a girl's pants, and I fell for it. Hell, I was barely in my twenties, then, and he was a handsome, rich guy, so I fell for it all. We broke it off after he hit my hand with that vase, though! I wasn't gonna be one of those women who keep getting out and then going back, not me. That was the end of that, and I was glad to be out of it!"

Sam thought for a minute. "Naturally, Jimmy is saying he's been framed, and that he's innocent, so we have to look into all these little things he's saying. Do you have any idea who might have hated Barry and Jimmy enough that they'd murder one and frame the other for doing it? Just assuming there's any truth to his claim, I mean, who do you think might be that kind of person?"

A flash of something dark went through her eyes, and she gave a derisive snort. "That little crack-whore of his might do something like that. What's her name, Janet? Janice, that's it. She might be that evil, if Jimmy was telling the truth, not that he is!"

Sam hesitated a moment. "Samantha, did you know that Barry and Janice got married a couple of months ago? They were keeping it a secret for the time being, but it's true."

The darkness hit again, but vanished after only a second. "Yeah, I knew. He told me right after, cause we'd been on-again, off-again lovers for a year or so, and he wanted me to know why he wasn't coming around anymore. He still came by once in a while to talk, though, just like that day. He said I had a level head on my shoulders, and he liked getting my opinions on stuff."

Sam nodded as if accepting it all. "Okay," he said. "Thanks for giving me your time, and helping me clear some of this up." He stood and turned toward the door. "One more question," he said. "Who else besides you knew that you'd gotten that message from Jimmy, warning you to stay out of his business?"

She thought for a second. "I told Bill about it after I got the hairs in the mail. Other than that, I don't think I told anyone." She paused. "You almost sound like you believe Jimmy."

Sam turned to her and shrugged his shoulders. "Something about this whole case is bugging me. It almost seems like it was too easy, and in my experience, when a case seems too easy it's because you missed something. I'm just trying to make sure nothing got missed."

"I don't think Jimmy is innocent," she said, "but if he is, then I hope you find whoever really did this. Barry deserves that, but I can tell you that it wasn't me, and I've told you the only other one I could think might do it. Even if they were married, there could be a thousand reasons why she'd turn on him, and there's just something about her that never sat right with me. You need to take a good look at her, I think."

Sam nodded. "I guarantee you, I'm going to. You're right; Barry deserves to have the truth come out, one way or another."

Sam left, then, and drove back toward his home. Since it was a Sunday morning, there wasn't a lot of traffic, and he spent the time thinking over all that he'd learned about the case.

Jimmy still seemed the most likely suspect, but if his wife was telling the truth, then he couldn't have done it. Samantha had been eager to come forward with the evidence she had, implicating him, but there was always the possibility that Jimmy was telling the truth and it was she who had called him from her phone, rather than Barry. The letter in the envelope containing the hairs had been typed, so anyone could have sent that to her, even she herself. Whoever did send it had been in possession of Barry's head at some point, and if that wasn't Jimmy, then it was someone who knew that Jimmy had called and left a threatening message on her phone, because they knew that her receiving the hairs would go along with that voicemail to implicate the agent. But according to Samantha, no one had known about it until after the envelope had been delivered.

The whole thing was like a 3-D jigsaw puzzle. Each piece left a place for a new piece, but the more pieces you had, the more complex the whole thing became and the harder it was to figure out the next piece.

His route home took him through some business districts, and he stopped to pick up a cup of coffee and a newspaper, then saw a store across the street that was open, and wandered inside. He spent a half hour there, browsing through their stock, and had to go back to the van to get some money from the bag. He made his purchase and left, smiling to himself.

He pulled into his driveway and parked the van next to Indie's old Taurus, looking over at it. With what was left of the money he'd just gotten from Mrs. Smith, Sam had a little over a hundred thousand dollars in cash lying around, and he thought that maybe some of it ought to go to buying her a better car. Every time she started that thing, it sounded like it was about to explode, and it had enough rust on it that he was expecting the cops to say it wasn't roadworthy any day.

He took the bag of money inside and found Indie sitting at her computer, just surfing the web, so he carried it into the bedroom and put it in his safe. When he came back to the dining room, she looked up at him.

"How did it go?" she asked.

He sat down beside her and set the bag on the table. "Well, I'm fifty thousand dollars richer, and probably twice as confused as I was before I got up this morning. No matter how I look at this case, there are parts that don't add up, and every time I get a statement from one person, someone else counters it, so at least one of them is lying, but I can't tell which one. Jimmy says it wasn't Barry who called him from Samantha's phone that day, but she swears it was. Whoever sent the hairs to her had to have known that Jimmy left a hateful message on her phone, but she says no one knew about it until after she got them. There's just no common thread I can follow through this thing."

Indie got up and began rubbing his shoulders. "You're tense," she said. "This thing is really getting to you."

"Yeah, cause I don't really believe Jimmy did it. Something about him killing Barry doesn't feel right; it'd be like the guy who killed the goose that laid the golden eggs. Barry was so good that sooner or later, some label was going to want him, and they'd let him bring the band along. Jimmy was the guy who could find that label, and even if he hated Chris with a passion, he still loves money. He'd have made the deal with Chris and the band in it before he'd have let all that money get away. Heck, he probably would have given in to Barry on it any day, just to get him to sign."

Indie wrapped her arms around him from behind and leaned her face down to kiss him. "There has to be an answer, and you'll find it. I know you will, Baby."

Sam held onto her arms, just feeling the goodness of her holding him.

"I hope so," he said. "I hope so."

10

Kenzie wouldn't be home until after dinner, so Sam and Indie would have most of the day to themselves. Sam decided he wanted a late breakfast, so they got into the Corvette and went to a diner he knew. They had eggs and bacon and hash browns, and Sam told Indie that he wanted to replace her car.

"We talked about that before," she said. "That car is all I've got left of Kenzie's father, Jared. I don't really want to get rid of it."

"I'm not saying you have to get rid of it, Babe. I was thinking we'd put it into the garage and start rebuilding it, but get you something else to drive so I know you and Kenzie are safer when you leave the house. The Taurus is in pretty rough shape, and when a car gets too rusty, it starts to get exhaust leaks and other problems that can be dangerous. I promise, we'll restore it completely, and one day when Kenzie is old enough to drive, you can give it to her."

Indie smiled at that thought. "That would be nice," she said. "Sam, she never knew him, but I've told her a little about him, and one day I'm sure she's gonna want to know more, even if we're together and she thinks of you as her Daddy. People always want to know where they came from, y'know? If we could give her his car one day, that would at least let her have a piece of him in her life, too. Does that make sense?"

Sam smiled. "Makes a lot of sense," he said, then changed the subject. "We've got all day to kill; what do you want to do?"

She laughed. "How about you surprise me?"

Sam smiled and said, "Okay, one big surprise, comin' right up!" He paid the check and they drove back home.

Indie smiled. "Is my surprise gonna be like your surprise last night?" she asked.

Sam laughed. "Not right at the moment," he said. He parked the van and got out, then opened the garage door and led her to the motorcycle. He handed her a helmet. "Have you ever been on a motorcycle?"

Indie grinned. "Not since high school, but yeah. Jared had one, but it wasn't as big as this. I've been wondering when you were gonna give me a ride, but it's hard to do when Kenzie's with us, I know." She slid the helmet over her head, and then Sam had to help her with the straps.

He backed the bike out and turned it around, then told her to climb on. When she was settled behind him, he pushed the starter button and they were off.

He took her out on I-70 and up into the mountains,

then took the Casino Parkway for the winding ride up through Black Hawk. Indie was holding on tight, her arms wrapped around his waist, but she grabbed even tighter when there were cliff walls alongside, some going up, and some showing drops of a hundred feet or more. Sam maneuvered the bike expertly through the curves and switchbacks, and they stopped in Black Hawk for lunch at the Main Street Restaurant.

Once they were seated, Indie said, "Okay, this is a blast! I haven't had so much fun in years! Sam, I had forgotten how much fun it can be just to get on a bike and ride!"

He smiled. "I had a feeling you'd like it," he said, "and I wanted us to get out of all our day-to-day stuff for a little while. Sometimes you just need a break, and I wanted to talk to you about something anyway, so I thought we might just get away for a little while."

"I'm lovin' it!" Indie said. "What did you want to talk about?" A waitress appeared suddenly, and Indie had to wait while they placed their orders. Both of them opted for burgers and fries, and the waitress said it would only be a few minutes. "So, again, what did you want to talk about?" Indie asked.

"Indie, I want to talk about us," Sam said, and the smile on his face was so bright that Indie suddenly felt her heart swelling. "I think last night changed things between us, and I want to know if you're feeling the same things I'm feeling."

Indie grinned. "I am, if you're feeling like we need to do that again!"

Sam laughed right out loud, and a few people turned to look at him. He got himself under control, and said, "I am, and again, and again! But at the moment I was referring to how you're feeling about us and our future together."

"Well," she said, "I wouldn't have gone where we went last night if I wasn't pretty sure we're right for each other. I mean—Sam, you're only the fourth man I've ever been with. Jared was first, and the last two were just out for—you know—and they vanished after they got it. So if I hadn't been sure you weren't gonna disappear on me, we never would have gone there."

Sam sat and stared at her for a moment. "I'd never do that to you," he said. "Indie, I'm not sure why, but I feel like there's something very special going on here. I know that when we're together, I feel complete, and when I'm away from you, I have to concentrate or I'll just be thinking about when I'll see you again. Sometimes I think about what would happen if you decided to move out, and it makes it hard to breathe, so I guess what I'm saying is that I seem to have become addicted to you. I feel good when I've got you, I jones for you when I don't, and I'm scared of the withdrawals if I had to give you up, so I figure you're my drug of choice!"

Indie's eyes went wide. "Wow, I've never been called a drug before," she said, "but I think I understand what you're saying. I feel the same way; the other night, before we talked, I was scared to death you were gonna say it wasn't working and I'd have to leave, and I thought I'd die if you did."

Sam took her hand across the table. "Then we're both on the same page, right? We both want to keep this together?"

Indie's breath was coming in short little bursts, and she was suddenly nervous. "Yes. We do."

Sam smiled. "Then let's make it official. I want to make sure I don't lose you, not ever, Indie. I want us to be together from now on."

Indie squeaked out, "Me, too."

"I know this is crazy, we've only known each other about three weeks, now, but I think I know enough to know what I want." He reached into a pocket and pulled out the item he'd purchased on his way home earlier, and held out a small box. When he opened it, Indie saw the beautiful diamond ring that was inside, and suddenly she could barely breathe at all. Sam took the ring out of the box and held it out to her as he got out of his chair and carefully dropped to one knee. "What I want is to make you and Kenzie my family. If this is too soon, I hope it won't scare you off, but—Indiana Perkins, will you marry me?"

Half the place was watching them, as Indie sat there and stared at the ring in his hand for more than a minute, without saying a word. Her hands were clasped tightly before her face, but then she extended her left hand out to Sam, and simply said, "Yes."

Sam slipped the ring on her finger, but it was a little too large, so he reached back into his pocket and took out a packet of little plastic things. "When I told the jeweler how tiny you are, he said these would help until I can bring you in to get it re-sized." He helped her fit one into the ring, and then slid it back on again, and this time it stayed in place.

Sam got up and so did Indie, and then she was in his arms and kissing him, and the whole place erupted in applause and cheers. Indie had to wave her hand around and show off the ring to all the ladies, and Sam got to shake hands and get his back slapped by most of the men. After a few moments, they were able to sit down again, and the waitress brought their food a minute later.

"The boss says this is on the house, kids," she said. "It isn't often we see something like that in here, so this is our gift to the two of you! Enjoy!"

Sam and Indie smiled as they ate their lunch, and she kept looking at the ring on her finger. "I can't wait to tell Kenzie," she said. "Do you—do you have an idea as to when you want to..." She trailed off.

"I want to get this case settled, first," Sam said, "and then I thought we'd look at a small ceremony with just family and good friends, then take a nice honeymoon somewhere special. Any idea where you'd like to go? Anywhere in the world?"

Indie smiled from ear to ear. "When I was younger," she said, "I used to dream about getting married and having a honeymoon in Mexico, but later I started thinking about having one in Hawaii. I've heard about people going there for a honeymoon, and how wonderful it all was. Do you think we could do that?"

"I think Hawaii would be perfect. We can certainly afford it, with all we've made this month, and if I can prove Jimmy didn't do it, we've got another fifty thousand coming. I've always thought of going to Hawaii, but never did. When Jeanie and I got married, our honeymoon was a weekend in Vegas, but we were young and not too smart; I want to do better by you."

Indie was still smiling. "I bet we could get Anita to keep Kenzie while we go. I love my daughter, don't get me wrong, but a honeymoon is a once-in-a-lifetime event, or—you know what I mean, and I don't think it's a good one to take kids along on."

Sam laughed. "I kind of agree with you on that," he said, "but we could always take a second honeymoon to Disney World, I'm sure she'd enjoy that."

"I've always wanted to take her there, but I never thought it would be possible. Do you really think we could do that?"

"I think we'll plan it for right after we get back from honeymoon number one, how would that be?"

Indie sat there and stared at him for several seconds, her burger in her hands and halfway to her mouth. "Sam

Prichard," she said, "I love you. It just hit me that we got engaged before either of us ever said that out loud."

Sam smiled. "I've said it to you a dozen times in my thoughts. Just didn't have the nerve to let it come out, but I can now. Indiana Perkins, I love you, and having you say yes has made me the happiest guy in the world!"

They finished eating and left the restaurant to a chorus of "Congratulations!" and "Best Wishes!" Indie put her helmet back on and climbed onto the back of the Shadow, and they rode back toward Denver by another route, this one with even more twists and curves than the last. Sam loved the laugh he heard from Indie when he powered the big bike through the curves, and knew that it was definitely a good day.

They got home a little after two, and still had several hours alone, so they put a couple of them to use in a very personal celebration of their engagement. Afterward, they lay together in bed, holding each other close and whispering about their love for one another. Sam said, "I don't know that I've ever really been in love before. I thought I was, when Jeanie and I got married, but I've gotta tell you, this feels so different and so much better; when she left, I didn't even get as upset about it as I thought I should have been. I think I was more in love with the idea of being in love than I was with her, does that make any sense?"

Indie nodded, and Sam felt it on his chest, where her head was lying. "I think I was in love with Jared," she said, "but this still feels different. It feels—I dunno, more grown up and mature, maybe, more real, somehow. I'm not saying what I had with Jared wasn't real; just, this is definitely not a bad thing."

Sam laughed and hugged her, then planted a kiss on the top of her head. "I know, Baby, I know. And I want you to know that I'm not a bit jealous of your feelings for Jared. Don't ever worry about talking to Kenzie about him, even right in front of me. I may become her Daddy, but he'll always be her father.

They got up after a while and took a shower, then went out into the living room and turned on the TV. There was a local news program on, and the announcer was talking about the murder. The scene cut to a shot of Jimmy's place, and the hole the police had found Barry's head and hands in.

Sam looked at the screen, and something in him twitched. He leaned forward and stared hard at it.

"What's the matter, Babe?" Indie asked, but Sam only shook his head.

"Not really sure, but look at that hole. It's right there next to the road, just like Jimmy said, but just across the street is a creek that's flowing pretty good. Now, if you were trying to get rid of body parts, would you bury them on your own property, or walk another twenty yards and toss them into a creek where they'd probably wash away and never turn up?"

Indie blinked. "You'd go for the creek. Anybody

would, it's just easier than trying to dig a hole and bury it."

"Right. Jimmy's telling the truth, Honey; someone is framing him for murder. Now all I gotta do is figure out who, and prove it."

"What about what Samantha said? Do you think there's any chance Janice could have done it?"

"Not unless she's an Oscar-worthy actress. She's a wreck without him, and that's pretty obvious. I don't think a real recovering addict could keep up an act like that for so long."

"Okay, then who else could have known about the phone message? That's sort of the key to solving it, don't you think? Whoever wanted to frame Jimmy had to know about that message, or there would have been no point in sending the hairs to her."

Sam nodded. "It's possible that it's just a coincidence that she got both the message and the hairs, but that would be a pretty big one. I'm inclined to think whoever killed Barry knew about the message, and wanted to use Samantha to bring the heat down on Jimmy. If we knew who else could have known about that message, we'd have a pretty good idea of how to proceed on this."

Indie got up and started for the dining room. "Let's talk to Herman for a bit," she said. "Maybe he can find something we're missing."

Sam followed her. "I don't know what it could be, but I'm ready to try your magic. What are you thinking?"

"If Herman can get into Jimmy's phone records, then we can see what time he made that call to Samantha's phone. We can then look at other calls he made, and see if we can get any idea who he might have told about it." She looked at him. "It stands to reason, doesn't it, that if she didn't tell anyone about the message, then maybe Jimmy did. Let's see who else he called around the same time."

Sam stopped where he was and stared at her. "Babe," he said, "have I mentioned today that I love you? That's a brilliant idea!"

Indie looked back at him over her shoulder. "Just part of my plan to keep you dependent on me, Baby, so you won't get cold feet and back out of marrying me! Let's see what Herman can do."

She sat down at her laptop and began tapping on the keys, and soon Herman was filling the screen with lines and lines of code that Sam couldn't tell from gibberish. Indie ran her finger over bits and pieces of it, then tapped more keys, and a moment later it all started again.

"What I'm doing is making Herman try all the different carriers to see who Jimmy's phone is with. We got it, here, he's on Verizon, and now Herman is trying to get into their billing computer. I've hacked it before, so it won't take long, and then we can look at his bill and see all of his call and text and data records."

Sure enough, the screen suddenly changed. A

browser opened to a Verizon page that showed Jimmy Smith's phone bill for the past month.

"Okay, Jimmy's got four phones on his account, probably his wife and kids have the other three. Here's the statement for his personal number." She clicked a link and another page opened up, with lines and lines of phone numbers with times and dates beside them, as well as how long each call had lasted. They looked for the Saturday two weeks prior, the day Barry disappeared, and found it.

"Okay, here's the call from Barry's phone, and here an hour and a half later is the one from Samantha Harris's phone. Check this out; the very next call Jimmy made was to Barry's phone. Now, why would he do that if he'd just talked to Barry on Samantha's?"

Sam nodded. "You're right, he wouldn't; he'd have called right back to hers and demanded to talk to Barry again."

"Let's keep going," Indie said. "Here's the next morning, and here's a call to Samantha's number. See that little double star next to the call? That means he used star six seven, to block the caller ID from showing who was calling. The call lasted eleven seconds, just long enough to leave the message, so that's the one we're looking for. Now, who did he call right after? He made three calls within the next ten minutes; let's find out whose numbers those are."

She switched to another screen and entered the

numbers, letting Herman do his thing. Less than a minute passed before there were three lines of information before their eyes.

"Check it out," Indie said. "The first call he made after leaving that message was to Bill Miller, less than a minute later, and it lasted four-and-a-half minutes. The second was to his wife, but that one only lasted a few seconds, and the third was about eight minutes later, to none other than Janice Peet, and it lasted almost four minutes. Kinda odd that neither Bill nor Janice ever mentioned those calls, isn't it?"

"Especially since they both knew I was looking at Jimmy Smith as a suspect. Telling me about them would have made me even more sure I was after the right guy, but they kept quiet. Curiouser and curiouser, said Alice. I think I need to visit them both in the morning, before Barry's funeral."

"Sam," Indie said, "when you go to see them, do me a favor, will you?"

"What's that, Honey?"

"Take your gun."

11

They spent the rest of the afternoon watching movies on television, until Kenzie came home at seven.

"She was a delight," Anita said, and her husband Jim added, "She's welcome anytime! The twins are delighted to have another kid their age in the neighborhood."

"Well, we appreciate it," Sam said, and then Indie showed Anita her ring, and the congratulations and hugs and backslapping began all over again. Kenzie jumped up and down when Indie told her that she and Sam were going to be getting married, and asked, "Now can he be my daddy?"

Sam picked her up and hugged her. "You bet I can, sweetheart!" he said, and that got him the biggest hug she'd given him yet.

Jim and Anita had to get back home, where her mother was watching their twins, so they said their goodbyes and left. Kenzie looked up at Sam after they were gone, and said, "Daddy?"

Sam smiled down at her. "Yes, Kenzie?"

She shrugged. "Nothing. I just wanted to say it." She turned and went to get Samson, who was sniffing around as if wondering what had changed while he was gone. Sam and Indie laughed as they watched her go.

"She's happy," Indie said. "She's wanted a daddy for a long time, and me telling her that her daddy was in heaven didn't help. She picked you even before I did, I think."

Sam looked at her. "Here's a question," he said. "Who all do we need to tell? I should call my mom and my sister, I guess, and Dan, and we'll tell the band tomorrow. What about you?"

Indie sighed. "I guess it's time I call my mom," she said. "I've been avoiding it for a while, because she always complains about how I live, but she doesn't want us staying with her, either. It's not that she doesn't love us, it's just—well, you'll get to know Mom, that's all I can say."

They sat down together at the dining room table, and Sam went first, calling his mother on speakerphone.

"Mom," he said, "it's Sam."

"Like I wouldn't know my own son's phone number when you call," she said, and Sam winced. "Even though I don't see it pop up on the phone very often, I still know it's you, cause it tells me it's you. To what do I owe the pleasure of you taking the time to call your old mother this time?"

Sam took a deep breath. "Well, Mom, I guess it's

because I'm getting married."

"Married? You're getting married? Is it that girl you told me about, the one who moved in and took over cleaning your house, so I don't get to come over and see my only son every week? Oh, I hope she's not like that one you were married to before, Sam, that woman was just never the right one for you, I do hope this one is better!"

"She's better, Mom, I promise, and yes, it's the same girl I told you about a few weeks ago. Her name is Indiana, and we call her Indie, and she's right here listening, I've got you on speaker."

"Well, hello, there, and what did you say her name was, was it Cindy?"

"No, Mom, it's Indie, short for Indiana, like in the movies with Indiana Jones. Indie."

"Hello, Indie, it's nice to talk to you, and don't believe half the things he says about me, I'm really not that bad! This is awfully quick, isn't it, Sam, I mean, you only told me she moved in with you what, a week ago? Two weeks? How can you be getting married so soon?"

"When it's right, Mom, it's just right, and Indie and I are very much right for each other. I just wanted you to know, and when we have a date set, we'll let you know that, too."

"Well, Sam, I have to say it's about time you found someone you really care for. You're just too nice a guy to be single, don't you think so, Indie?"

Indie laughed. "Yes, Ma'am, I sure do!"

"Oh, my God, what's with this 'ma'am' stuff, we can't have that! I'm just 'Mom,' sweetheart, let's keep it simple. Oh! Wait a minute, Sam, you told me she had a little girl! Does this mean I finally have a grandchild? That's it, I'm coming over! I'll be there in an hour!" The line went dead instantly.

Sam looked at Indie sheepishly. "Mom's got a memory like an elephant, I'm afraid, and she never forgets anything! She's been begging me and my sister to make her a grandmother for as long as I can remember, so she's gonna latch onto Kenzie as fast as she can!"

Indie smiled. "Don't worry, Kenzie will have her wrapped around her little finger in no time flat!"

Sam dialed again, and called his sister. "Carrie, it's Sam," he said when she answered, and his sister responded with delight.

"Sam? And you're calling me? Uh-oh, Buddy, what kind of trouble are you in now?" Indie could hear the smile in her voice.

"No trouble," he said. "I just thought you'd want to know that your big brother is gonna be getting married soon. I just got off the phone from telling Mom, and wanted you to be the next to know."

Carrie squealed through the phone line. "*Married? You're getting married?* Okay, tell me everything, like who is she, and how long have you known her and *everything!*"

Sam laughed. "Her name is Indiana, and she goes by Indie, just like Indiana Jones, and she's gorgeous and has a beautiful four-year-old daughter named Mackenzie, but we call her Kenzie for short. We've known each other about three weeks, but it's been the most intense three weeks you can imagine, and we just came to the conclusion today that we're right for each other, and this is what we want. We don't have a date yet, but we'll let you know as soon as we do so you can come to the wedding. Say hi, I've got you on speaker."

"Oh, hi, Indie! I'm Carrie, Sam's little sister, and I'm not nearly as bad as he'll tell you I am, well, maybe I am, but it's all good, anyway, right? Oh, my goodness, this is so exciting! And you've got a little girl? Mom will go absolutely crazy over that!"

"Yeah," Sam said, "she's actually on the way here right now. If I know her, she's probably gonna get a speeding ticket on the way."

Carrie laughed. "Yeah, probably! Indie, tell me all about it! How did you guys meet?"

Sam looked at Indie and let her take the conversation. "Well, he actually ran across me when he needed help with something, and me and my little girl were not doing so well. We were actually homeless, and Sam had this big old house, so he said we could stay with him for a while, and the more we were around each other, the more we just knew there was something special going on. I knew I was in love with him a week ago, and today he surprised me with a ring and popped the question, and I said yes. Kenzie is so happy she's about to burst; she's been wanting him to be her daddy since the day we met him, I think."

"Oh, I can tell already we're gonna get along great! If there's one thing I love, it's being impulsive, and if you guys are getting married this fast then you're probably as impulsive as I am! I can't wait to meet you! Are you on Facebook?"

The two girls exchanged Facebook info and promised to friend each other, then Sam managed to get them off the phone. He called Dan and told him, and that set off another round of excitement. He said he'd spread the word around the PD the next day, and that he'd better be on the list for Best Man. Sam promised him that he was at the top of that short list, and they ended the call.

Then it was Indie's turn. She said she had very few friends, and most of those were only on Facebook, so all she needed to do was call her mother. She dialed the number nervously, and like Sam, she put it on speaker.

"Hello?" came a voice that was surprisingly similar to Indie's.

"Hey, Mom," Indie said.

"Indiana? Hey, Sweetie, how are you? Where are you? I haven't heard from you in weeks! Are you okay? Is Kenzie okay?"

"Yes, Mom, we're fine. I'm actually calling to tell you

some good news. Are you sitting down?"

"Good news? I can stand some of that! Yes, I'm sitting down, go ahead."

Indie took a beep breath of her own. "Mom—I'm getting married."

"Married?" her mother echoed, incredulous. "Did you just say you're getting married?"

Indie laughed. "Yes, Mom, I said I'm getting married. I've met a wonderful man who loves me and Kenzie, and we just adore him, and he's asked me to marry him. His name is Sam, and he's a private investigator. We met when I went to work for him." She held a finger to her lips to tell Sam to be quiet.

"Oh, that's wonderful, Indie! But when did this happen? The last I heard from you, you were homeless and out of work!"

"Um—well, about three weeks ago, Sam needed some help with something, and I answered an ad he put out, and when he found out we were living in shelters, he said he had a big house with extra rooms, and let us stay with him, and we just—hit it off. I really love him, Mom, and he loves us. This is a good thing."

Her mother was quiet for a moment, and then said, "Yes, I can feel that it is. This Sam is a good man, and he'll be a good husband." Sam raised his eyebrows, and Indie signaled to wait, that she'd tell him later, but her mother blew that. "You did tell him about Beauregard, didn't you?"

"Um, well, I hadn't quite got around to that yet. You're on speaker, Mom, Sam can hear you."

"Hello, Mrs. Perkins," Sam said.

"Well, hello, Sam! I am so happy for Indie that she's found you! Beauregard says you're a great man, and that he knew you in a past life, when you fought at Valley Forge together! He says you'll make a wonderful husband to my daughter, and a terrific father for little Mackenzie!"

Sam looked at Indie, who made pleading eyes at him. "Well," he said, "I don't remember that, but tell Beauregard I said thank you for the endorsement!"

"He says you're welcome, and most people don't remember their past lives, so it's okay. He says not to worry, you'll know him again one day; he's scheduled to be reborn sometime in the next year or so."

Sam's eyebrows went up another notch. "Oh, well, that's great, then," he said, looking at Indie for guidance.

"Well, anyway, Mom, I just wanted to let you know, and when we get a date set, I'll let you know that, too. We'll make sure to send you an invitation!"

"Okay, sweetie," her mother said. "I'll keep you both in my meditations!"

"Bye, Mom," Indie said, and cut the call off before her mother could say anything else.

She looked sheepishly at Sam. "I probably should have warned you about that," she said, "but I was sort of hoping she wouldn't mention Beauregard this soon.

Sometimes she doesn't, 'til she gets to know you better."

"Uh-huh," Sam said. "And Beauregard would be..."

"Remember I told you Mom was sort of a throwback hippie? Well, she's into a lot of new age stuff, and Beauregard is her, um—her spirit guide. She says he's an old soldier from the civil war, but he tells her about a lot of other past lives too. And he seems to know a lot about just about everyone, because she always says he knew someone in a past life somewhere along the line. You're lucky he didn't say he knew you during Roman times, or even in the dark ages. Valley Forge is at least part of American history."

Sam looked at her for a minute. "And do you have a spirit guide?"

She rolled her eyes at him. "No! I've never bought into that crap, not even when I was a kid!" Then she shrugged. "Although, I can say that there have been times when Beauregard's told her things that turned out to be right. She says he told her that I'd never be married to Jared, even though he thought Jared was a great guy, too. All he would say was that something would keep us from ever being married, and he turned out right about that."

"You sound like you almost believe in him."

Indie shrugged again. "I don't, not really. I think maybe my Mom has a touch of second sight or whatever you want to call it, but I think Beauregard is just a figment of her warped imagination, y'know? He's the way she deals with things she knows that she doesn't understand how she knows."

"Well, as long as he likes me, I think we'll try to stay on his good side, right?" A car pulled into the driveway, then, and they heard a door open and close. Sam closed his eyes for a second. "That would be Mom," he said, and got up to go to the door. Indie called Kenzie to come back in from the back yard.

"Sam!" his mother said as she came onto the porch and found him standing there. "Sam, you've made me the happiest mother on earth! I just couldn't wait another minute to come and meet this wonderful girl and your new daughter!"

Sam gave her a hug. "Come on in, Mom, Indie's inside with Kenzie." She followed him in, and they found Indie in the living room, holding Kenzie in her arms.

"Indie, Kenzie, this is my mother, Grace; Mom, this is Indie and Mackenzie, but we call her Kenzie for short."

His mother threw her arms open and wrapped both girls in a hug. "Oh, my God, I'm so glad to meet you both! This is a dream come true to an old woman!"

"Mom!" Sam said. "You're not even fifty yet!"

"But I feel sixty, so it counts!" She let them go and stood back, looking at both of them. Kenzie was smiling widely, but Indie's smile was a little nervous. "Oh, what a preciously adorable little girl! Indie, I hope you understand, dear, but I've wanted to be a grandma forever, and so I'm planning to spoil this child completely rotten, is that okay? Because if it's not, then you're just marrying into the wrong family, sweetheart, that's just how it is! Kenzie, I'm gonna be your new Grandma, is that okay with you?"

Kenzie smiled and said, "Yes!" and then surprised both Indie and Sam by reaching her arms out to Grace, who squealed with delight and took her from Indie. "Oh, Sam, she's wonderful, they both are! You are such a lucky man, Samuel Prichard, to have found this wonderful young woman and gotten the chance to bring them both into your life! Don't you ever forget to count your blessings, young man, and I mean don't you ever forget it!"

Sam chuckled. "Trust me, Mom, I won't! And I know just how lucky I am to have both of them!"

Grace took Kenzie to the couch and sat down, holding the little girl on her lap. Kenzie showed no sign of wanting down, so they sat there together, Kenzie on her new Grandma's lap, while Sam and Indie sat together on the love seat across the room.

"Okay, tell me everything," Grace said, and Sam and Indie looked at each other in confusion for a second. Grace cleared it up by adding, "I want her clothing sizes, her shoe size, what her favorite colors are, what kind of toys she likes, all of it! This is my first grandkid, and I plan to enjoy myself! Or can I just come get her sometime and take her to the mall? Would that be alright?"

Indie looked at Sam, and he nodded with a grin. "Sure, yeah," she said. "I'm sure Kenzie would love it, but don't let her get away with too much..."

"Nonsense, there's no such thing as too much for a first grandchild! One of the joys of being a grandma is that I get to take the child out and buy her goodies, then bring her home and let you deal with the aftermath!"

"Mom," Sam began, but Indie stopped him.

"Sam, it's okay, I know what she means," she said with a grin. "My mother always said the same thing."

"Of course it's okay, mothers understand these things, don't they, Indie?" Grace turned her attention to Kenzie. "So, tell me, Kenzie, what kind of things do you like to do?"

Kenzie thought for a minute. "I like to go to the zoo," she said, "and I like to play with Samson."

"Oh, is Samson your doggie?" Grace asked, but Samson picked that very moment to come running into the room, which naturally resulted in him tumbling halfway across the living room floor. When he came to a stop, he shook his head like always, then stood up and looked around. When he spotted Kenzie sitting on Grace's lap, he walked over and jumped up to join her.

Kenzie said, "This is Samson! He's a kitty cat!" She started petting Samson, who immediately began to purr.

"I see that," Grace said, "and a very nice kitty cat he

is!" She looked at Sam. "Does he always fall like that? Is he okay?"

"That's normal for our Samson, Mom, he's fine. He just has a problem getting his back legs to work with his front legs when he's running."

Grace looked at Kenzie, then at Samson, then up to Indie and Sam. "I've got to say it, Sam," she said. "You've got yourself a beautiful little family here. Dare I hope that there will be more children in the future?"

Sam and Indie looked at each other, both realizing that they hadn't discussed how either of them felt about having more kids. Indie smiled at him and turned back to Grace.

"I think so," she said. "I want more kids, and Sam needs kids of his own, as well as Kenzie, don't you think?"

Grace looked at Sam with a huge smile. "Samuel!" she said. "Why couldn't you have found this one before you ever met that other one?"

Sam looked at Indie and grinned. "Um, well, Mom, that might not have worked out, cause Indie would have been about thirteen, then, and I'm not sure how her mother would have taken to her dating a cop who was twenty-one."

"Good point, but at least you found her now! And Grandma is just so happy she could cry," she said, aiming it at Kenzie, "yes, she is!"

Kenzie giggled, and hugged her, and then Grace

suddenly did have tears in her eyes. She looked at her son and said, "I am so proud of you, Sam, and your father would be, too."

12

Sam and Indie put Kenzie to bed after Grace left, and spent some time alone in the living room. Sam sat on the couch with Indie cuddled up to him the way they had gotten used to, and they watched a bit of TV together, but their minds weren't on the show.

"So, you do want more kids?" Sam asked.

"Uh-huh. Do you?"

"I do," he said. "I can't believe we didn't talk about that at some point."

"I'm sure we would have gotten to it soon," Indie said. "Your mom doesn't pull any punches, does she?"

Sam laughed. "Not Mom, no. Whatever she's thinking tends to fall right on out of her mouth! That's one of the things you just have to get used to, with her."

"Well, at least it's her own thoughts, and not Beauregard's. I can live with it, trust me! And did you see how Kenzie took to her? That child normally needs at least a couple of days to get used to anyone, but she actually reached for your mom! I was shocked!"

"Yeah, I was half afraid Mom would be so over-exuberant that it would scare Kenzie off, but it didn't turn out that way. I'm glad; she and Mom will get long good, I think."

They sat together in silence for a few minutes, and then Indie asked the question they were both thinking about. "So—what do you want to do about, um—sleeping arrangements? Do you want me to move on in with you, or should I stay upstairs for now? I mean, Kenzie's in her own room, now, so it isn't like she needs me up there..."

Sam grinned. "Well, I'd be a liar if I said I didn't want you with me," he said, "but the one we have to consider is Kenzie. How do you think she'll handle it if you move downstairs?"

"I sort of asked her how she'd feel if I moved down with you when I put her to bed," Indie said, "and she said, 'Don't mommies and daddies have to sleep together?' Sometimes I think she's a lot older than she pretends to be. Anyway, I said that sometimes they do, and she said it was okay with her. I just didn't know how you'd feel about it, when we're not actually married, yet."

Sam smiled down at her. "Baby, I would love it if you wanted to be with me, and not just for the obvious reasons. I like waking up with you beside me, and I love the feeling of someone snuggled up beside me. Are you okay with it?"

She nodded against his chest. "Yeah, I am. I liked

being with you last night, and I woke up this morning after you left, and I cried, because I thought it was something that might only happen once, or maybe only now and then. I wanted to tell you when you got home that I was in love with you, but I was afraid I'd scare you, or make you pull back from me, so I didn't say anything. But I wanted to move down and be with you, I did. I still do, and now I can."

"We'll worry about the moving tomorrow. For tonight, we'll just wing it. You might want to go up and get anything you want to sleep in, though, because I suspect the bedroom door won't necessarily keep Miss Kenzie out anymore."

"Um, yeah, you're probably right. I'll be right back." She got up and went upstairs, coming back down a few moments later with a nightgown and her bathroom things, and went into Sam's room. He rose and turned off the TV, then followed her. She was in the bathroom, putting her things away, and he walked over to the door there and watched her.

"This is nice," he said. "This place has needed a woman's touch forever. You can redecorate in here, if you want to. Shower curtain, all that stuff, even in the bedroom. Heck, you can redecorate the whole house, if you want to. None of the stuff that's here was Jeanie's, so it's not that her touch is on any of it, but you can do it however you want."

She smiled at him. "Well, the shower curtain is kinda

mildewy, and I guess I could see a few changes I'd like to make. You sure that's okay?"

He stepped inside and pulled her into his arms. "Indie, this is your home now, too. I want you to make it the way you want it. I'm not one of those guys who can't sleep under a frilly blanket, Babe."

She leaned against him and put her own arms around him. "I love you, Sam."

"I love you, too, Indie. Let's go to bed. I'm still sore from last night, and the bike ride didn't make it any better."

They got into sleeping clothes and climbed into bed. A couple hours later, they went to sleep in each other's arms.

Sam woke up at eight, to the alarm they'd set the night before. Indie was already up and out of bed, and he took a fast shower and dressed, then found her making breakfast in the kitchen. Kenzie was up, too, and sitting on the floor with Samson. She looked up at him and said, "Hi, Daddy!" and Sam broke into a smile.

"Hello, Baby girl!" he said. "How's my princess this morning?"

"I'm fine," she said. "Mommy sleeps down here with you now."

"Um, yeah, I know. Is that okay with you?"

"Uh-huh," she said, nodding. "All my friends who have mommies and daddies told me their mommies and daddies sleep together, so I know that's how it's 'posed to be." She went back to making the cat dance on his back paws, and he seemed to be enjoying it.

Sam walked over to where Indie was stirring pancake mix and slipped his arms around her from behind. "Hello, my big Baby girl," he whispered into her ear, and she shivered.

"Do you have any idea what you do to me when you whisper into my ear?" she asked him. "Makes me want to drag you right back into that bedroom!"

"I'm good with that, but we better wait 'til Kenzie isn't around. Might give the poor kid a complex if she saw her mommy dragging her daddy, y'know?" He kissed her ear, which made her shiver again, and then went to pour himself some coffee, taking it to the table. He sat down and took a long sip of it, and smiled from ear to ear.

When the pancakes were ready, Sam told Kenzie to get up to the table and helped her get her chair situated the way she wanted it, then helped her get the butter and syrup onto her short stack. Indie joined them a second later, and asked Kenzie to say grace.

"Thank you, God, for this breakfast, and for my new daddy and for Samson and for making mommy smile so much. Oh, and thank you for my new Grandma! Amen!"

Sam and Indie said, "Amen!" and then looked at each other and fought back the giggles that wanted to come out of them both. If Kenzie had noticed Indie smiling more, then they might need to be a little less obvious.

They ate their breakfast and talked about the things they were going to do for the day. Sam said he had a couple of people he wanted to see, and then he wanted to take Indie out car shopping, and Indie said she wanted to go and get some groceries and things for the bathroom. Kenzie wanted to know if she could get a new doll, one that could talk and move and do all this neat stuff that she saw on TV, and Sam said it was okay with him if she could talk her mommy into it. Indie glared at him with mock ferocity, but then pretended to give in after a half dozen cries of "please" from both Kenzie and Sam.

Sam put his Glock into its holster and strapped it onto his belt, then left shortly after breakfast and went to Bill Miller's apartment. When he rang the bell, Miller answered, looking half awake.

Sam couldn't help staring for a moment. Knowing that the man standing in front of him was really a woman, he could see certain characteristics that should have been obvious the first time they met. Miller had no Adam's Apple, his skull was shorter than it would be if he were genetically male, and the first fingers of each hand were slightly longer than the third fingers. Each of these was a common indicator that police were trained to spot when dealing with gender impersonators, but Sam had missed them.

"Mr. Prichard," Miller said. "What can I do for

you?"

"I'm trying to wrap up some details about Barry's death, and wondered if we could talk for a few more moments?"

Miller shrugged. "Sure, come on in. Give me a minute and I'll put coffee on."

Sam went in and sat on the couch again, and waited for a few minutes. Miller came back with two cups of coffee on the same tray, and Sam kicked himself again, mentally. Men don't often use serving trays, preferring to carry extra items like sugar and cream in a separate trip. Miller set the tray down, and Sam added sugar to his coffee.

"So how can I help?" Miller asked.

"Well, there have been a few things coming up that aren't fitting in so well, and I'm hoping you can help me make sense of them. For instance, you know that Jimmy Smith was arrested for the murder, right?"

"Yeah, and I can't say I was terribly surprised."

"Well, it turns out that he left a nasty message on Samantha Harris's voicemail the day after Barry disappeared, and when he was asked who else he called that day, he said he called you. Can you tell me what the call was about?"

Miller looked at him warily for a second. "I'm afraid he must be lying, Mr. Prichard. Jimmy Smith and I don't talk, and he'd have no reason to call me."

Sam sat there for a moment and wondered why he'd

just been lied to. "Mr. Miller—or should I actually be saying Miss Miller? I've seen Jimmy Smith's phone logs, and it clearly shows a call to your cell phone that lasted four-and-a-half minutes, not even a minute after he left that message on Samantha's phone. Now, can we get past the BS and into some truth here?"

There was silence for a moment, and then a tear appeared on Miller's cheek. "No one has mentioned that in so long that I had hoped I'd never have to talk about it again. It's not really a matter of 'miss' or 'mister,' I'm afraid, Mr. Prichard. I am actually a hermaphrodite, both male and female. My mother couldn't deal with that inconvenient truth, and so I was raised as a girl. It wasn't until I was raped and became pregnant that it truly mattered to me, and once the child was born, I chose to comport myself as a man from then on."

Sam cocked his head to one side. "But according to records, Barry Wallace was the child's father. Are you saying Barry raped you?"

"No. Barry wasn't the kind of man who could do such a thing. Instead, he was the kind who would take the responsibility and help me cover up that horrible night, by saying that he and I had gotten drunk and made a mistake, which left me with child. When the baby was born, his name was listed as the father, but it wasn't really his."

"Then whose was it?" Sam asked.

Miller only looked at him. "It was a gang rape, Mr.

Prichard. I had been invited to a party with a bunch of the more popular kids, and I went. Somewhere during the evening, someone slipped a drug into one of my drinks, and as far as I can remember, there were no fewer that a dozen who had me that night. I have no idea who some of them were, and I simply couldn't bear to tell anyone what had happened, so I called the one real friend I had, and that was Barry. He came and got me and helped me clean myself up, then took care of me through the rest of that night, while I wept and screamed and even beat on him as a representative of the males of the species." He sniffled and wiped his nose with a napkin from the tray. "Of course, some of those who had done it told, and soon the word was out that I had both sets of sexual organs, a vagina and a small but definite penis. People began to shun me, and that's part of the reason I've been able to live here again; those who knew me have done their best to forget me, and I look very different as a man than I did as a woman."

"Miller, I'm sorry. But I still need to know about that phone call."

Miller sat there and looked at the floor for several seconds, and Sam merely waited. After almost a minute, Miller said, "Jimmy called me. Jimmy Smith is one of the very few people who know the truth about me, and about what happened that night, because he was the agent who had bought the first song I ever sold, one that Barry and I had written together. When I called Barry that night, he was with Jimmy Smith, and Jimmy brought him to pick me up." He sniffled once again, and used the napkin. "My clothes were torn so badly that there wasn't enough left to cover myself with, so Jimmy took off his jacket and wrapped it around me, and he paid for the motel room where Barry cleaned me up and took care of me. He even went and got antiseptic lotions and such, to help, and he never told anyone about it, but I've avoided ever having to face him again, since then. Barry always dealt with him when he wanted one of my songs, so I wouldn't have to. He knew that Barry and I were still close friends, despite the public stuff that said we hated each other, so he figured if anyone knew where Barry was, it'd be me."

"Then, you had reason to believe Jimmy was innocent. I'm curious why you didn't come forward."

"And have to explain how I know so much? I'd have to relive that night all over again, and if you think telling you about it was hard just now, imagine what I'd be like if I had to tell it in court. Do you think a prosecutor wouldn't use it to tear me up on the stand, make it sound like I was lying because I was loyal to Jimmy for his help that night? No, thank you. Jimmy did me a favor, yes, but I've paid it back many times in other ways. He's on his own with this one."

Sam looked at him and thought about what he'd just heard. "Tell me something else. Assume someone hated Barry enough to kill him, and hated Jimmy enough to frame him; who would you think it would be?"

Miller thought about it, Sam could tell, but then shook his head. "See, the first half of that is the problem," he said, "because I can't imagine anyone ever hating Barry. He was just the absolute nicest guy you'd ever want to know, and he'd give you or anyone else the shirt off his back. I can't imagine who could hate him, not at all. Jimmy? Lots of people hate Jimmy, and not all of them are former clients. He's never been close to anyone who didn't end up hating his guts, and I do mean not anyone! If they've known Jimmy Smith for more than a few months, they hate him for one reason or another." He wiped his nose once more. "How strange is it that the only two people he ever knew who didn't hate him would be me and Barry? And neither one of us can help him."

"One last question, and it's about your child: did you know that Barry and Janice Peet got married, and that he was trying to take the little girl back from his sister?"

Miller's eyes went wide, and Sam knew the answer instantly. "No! He'd never said a word, not about getting married, and not about trying to get Abbie back! I had no idea, but I can tell you this, his sister will never let that little girl go. She couldn't have kids of her own, and when Barry said he had a child he couldn't raise, she jumped up to adopt her, and she's been very, very good for her. But give her up? If Barry was trying that, you might want to find out where she and her husband were the night he died."

"Then they know that you were the mother?"

"Yes, but it was all sealed in the adoption records. I'll say it again, Mr. Prichard; if Barry was trying to take that little girl away from Marjorie and Philip, I wouldn't be a bit surprised if they killed him. Abbie's their one and only reason for living."

Sam left, completely blown away by everything he'd heard. Could it be possible that the killer was Barry's own sister, or his brother-in-law? He called Indie.

"Babe, it's too long to go into over the phone, but I need an address for Barry Wallace's sister, Marjorie and her husband. At the moment, they may be my top suspects in this mess."

"Wow," she said. "Hang on a minute and I'll have it for you."

A minute later, Sam punched the address into his GPS and headed off into Arvada to find Barry's sister. He had a gut feeling that he was getting close to the real solution to the case, and wanted to bring it to a close as soon as he could.

He parked in front of the house and walked up to knock, but the door opened before he could raise his hand. A woman stood there, and he recognized her from the news story.

"Mrs. Newcomb? My name is Sam Prichard, I'm a private investigator hired to look into your brother's death. I was wondering if I could ask you a few questions."

She narrowed her eyes at him. "Who hired you?"

she asked.

Sam smiled. "Ma'am, that's confidential, and I'm not at liberty to answer that question, but I've come across some information that makes me think we really ought to talk."

"I don't think I have anything to say to you, Mr..."

"Ma'am, you can talk to me and help me clear this up, or I have to turn it all over to the police, and let them come talk to you. Since some of it involves your daughter, I thought you might prefer to deal with me."

Marjorie froze for a second, and then opened the screen door wide. "Come on," she said stiffly, and let Sam enter, then led him into the living room of the house. A little girl of about twelve was sitting at a table in the adjacent dining room. Marjorie said, "Abbie, I've got to talk some business with this gentleman, Honey, so I want you to go up to your room for a while."

"Yes, Ma'am," the girl said, and picked up her things and walked up the stairs.

"Please have a seat, Mr. Prichard," Marjorie said, and Sam sat down on a chair, while she sat on the sofa. "Now, what is this all about?"

"I know all the details behind your adoption of your little girl, Mrs. Newcomb, even the ones that are sealed. I also know that your brother was trying to take her back from you, and that you were dead set against that happening. I've also been told that you made threats about seeing Barry in hell first, and that you would send anyone who tried to help him there as well, at gunpoint."

"That's ridiculous," she said. "I've never said any such thing."

"Mrs. Newcomb, Jimmy Smith is half convinced that you killed your brother and set him up to take the fall for it. If he goes on a lie detector and tells about his confrontation with you, I think you're gonna be trying to explain it to police detectives, not just me."

Marjorie sat there and stared at him for twenty seconds. "Fine, that bastard Smith came out here and tried to convince me to let Barry have her back! He got pushy, and I lost my temper, and I grabbed my gun out of my purse and told him that if he didn't leave, I'd shoot him. And before you ask, yes, I have a concealed carry permit."

"That doesn't matter to me, I have one, too. What I want to know is the last time you actually saw Barry and talked to him."

"The last time I saw him was almost a month ago, when we met at my attorney's office to explain that the adoption is sealed, and can't be reopened. He got angry and said that he and his new wife would be better for Abbie, and I said it was ridiculous to rip a child away from the only family she's ever known, and try to force her to accept a new one. He threw the papers he had at me, and stormed out the door, and I never saw him again." She sighed. "The last time I talked to him, however, was the day he disappeared. He called me and said he'd been thinking about what I said, and that I was right; that taking Abbie away from us and trying to make her understand that he was her father would only confuse her and cause her problems, so he was going to drop the lawsuit. We made up that day, and talked for about an hour, the first time we'd really talked in weeks. I even invited him to come to her dance recital the next week, and when he didn't show up, I got angry and thought he was going to start playing games; I didn't know we'd never see him alive again."

Sam looked at her for a moment, trying to read her body language, but nothing about her seemed to indicate she was lying. He thanked her for her time and left, and called Indie as soon as he got into the van.

"Can you still get into Barry's phone records?" he asked, and she said, "Sure. What do you need?"

"Tell me if he called his sister the day he vanished."

"Gimme a minute," she said, and he could hear her tapping keys. "Yep," she said a moment later. "He called her about an hour before his call to Jimmy Smith."

"How long did the call last?" Sam asked.

"Hmm. Fifty-two minutes."

Sam thought. "That doesn't sound like a call where people are angry and hateful, does it? According to his sister, he called her that morning to say he'd decided to drop his suit to take the little girl, because he'd come to understand that it would be a shock to her; the Newcombs are the only parents she's ever known, and she has no idea that Barry is supposed to be her father. To be honest, I believe she's telling the truth."

"And you don't think Miller is involved?"

"Well, not in any way that's criminal, no."

"Then that only leaves Janice, doesn't it?"

Sam sighed. "Yeah, and that's where I'm going next. I'll call you when I get done there."

Sam pulled up to Janice's apartment building forty minutes later, and rang the bell to let her know someone was there. Her voice came over the intercom a moment later.

"Yes?"

"Janice, it's Sam Prichard. Can I come up and talk to you for a few minutes?"

The door buzzed and let him in, and he took the elevator up to the third floor, where her apartment was. He found it and tapped lightly on the door, and she let him in.

"Have a seat," she said, pointing to the kitchen table and chairs. The apartment was an efficiency, with only a small bedroom, a bath and a kitchen, so he sat where she indicated. "What can I do for you, Sam?"

"The day Barry disappeared, Jimmy Smith called you. Can you tell me what it was about?"

"Jimmy? Jimmy didn't call me, not that day. I mean, I've talked to him before, but not that day."

Sam sighed. "Janice, I saw his phone records, and

they show that he did call your phone that day. It was just a little while after he called Samantha Harris and left that voicemail."

Janice seemed to brighten a bit. "Oh, his *phone*! Yeah, I got a call from his phone, but it wasn't Jimmy."

She stopped, and Sam looked at her, exasperated. "Well, if it wasn't Jimmy, then who was it?"

"Oh. It was his wife, I think her name was Sheila."

Sam rolled his eyes. "She called you from Jimmy's phone? Did she say what she wanted?"

"Oh, yeah, she wanted to know if Jimmy had been over here lately. See, me and Jimmy had a little thing a couple years back, and she hates me. She called me to see if he'd been coming to see me again, and I told her no, and that I wasn't interested in seeing him, either. I didn't tell her me and Barry got married, but I said we were talking about it."

Sam's mind began to race. "And you're sure that was when she called you? That it wasn't Jimmy who called?"

She nodded emphatically. "Yeah, I'm sure. She was all mean and everything, really mad about something, and I didn't know what, but then she said he'd been talking to Sammie Harris, and I guess she just thought he'd been calling some of his old girlfriends. She said if I ever saw him again, she'd come after me, but I just told her to get a life, y'know? I didn't need that crap."

Sam sat there and thought it all through for a moment, then got up and thanked her. He let himself out and started down the hall to the elevator.

Things were starting to make some sense, but he wasn't sure if it was any kind of sense he could put together and prove. He needed one more piece of information before he could be sure of what he was thinking, and that was at the county jail.

It took him another thirty minutes to get there, and he hurried in and said he needed to see Jimmy Smith. The jailer on duty told him to wait a minute, then called another to take him back. He was seated in the same interview room, and a minute later Smith was brought in.

"Sam," Smith said with a grin. "Can I hope you've got some good news?"

"I'm not sure yet, Jimmy, but I think I'm onto something. I need to ask you a question, though. The day you called and left the voicemail for Samantha Harris, right after that, you made some other calls. Can you remember who else you called?"

Smith hesitated for a second, but then he shrugged. "I called a guy named Bill Miller, he's a friend of Barry's. I figured if anyone might be able to get Barry to talk to me, he could."

Sam nodded. "And after that?"

Smith scrunched up his face in concentration. "I don't remember calling anyone else, after that. I went to get something from my office, and remember I left my phone at the house."

"According to your phone records, right after you

called Miller, you called your wife, but the call only lasted a few seconds."

Smith's face lit up. "Oh, yeah," he said. "I called Sheila, cause I thought she was out shopping, but she was there at the house. When I called her I heard her phone ring, and I turned around and she was just coming into my den, so I hung up and told her I had to run to the office for a few minutes. I thought I'd put my phone in my pocket, but I must have set it down without thinking, and left it."

Sam leaned forward. "Jimmy," he said, "think about this: how long was she right behind you?"

Smith sat there and stared at him. "I don't know," he said after a few seconds. "I thought she was just coming in, but she might have been there for a few minutes, I don't know. Why?"

Sam shook his head. "Never mind that, tell me this," he said. "Who else knew about the message you left on Samantha's voicemail?"

Smith scrunched his face again. "Well, no one that I can think of. Sam, why are these questions so important?"

"Jimmy, if they are, I'll know it soon, and I can tell you then. For right now, though, don't tell anyone, and I mean not *anyone*, that I asked them! I'll be back in touch pretty soon—but I think we just caught a break— sort of."

Sam called for the jailer and left, thinking through

everything that he had learned. He'd been after one piece of information for the past two days, and he finally thought he had it, but there was one thing that still didn't fit in. He had an idea of who had framed Jimmy; the only remaining question was how that person had come into possession of Barry's head and hands. He had to find that out to make it all work and nail the killer.

13

Sam pulled up in front of Jimmy Smith's house about forty-five minutes later, and rang the doorbell. Mrs. Smith answered after a few moments, and smiled at him. "Mr. Prichard," she said. "Is it good news, I hope?"

"Actually, it is, Mrs. Smith," Sam said. "I'm pretty sure I'm going to be able to prove that Jimmy was framed, but I need your help with it."

She looked excited. "Certainly, just tell me how! Won't you come in, where we can talk more comfortably?" She held the door wide and Sam stepped in, then followed her to the living room and they sat on the couch.

"Mrs. Smith, I've got an idea of who framed your husband for the murder of Barry Wallace, but I need you to help me figure out a few details."

She looked a little confused. "Details? I don't know how I can help, but I'm willing to try."

Sam smiled. "Good, because the one thing I can't figure out is how you killed Barry Wallace."

Sheila Smith's eyes went wide instantly. "How *I* killed him? Mr. Prichard, what on earth would make you think I would, or even *could* do something like that?"

"Mrs. Smith, someone sent an envelope containing some of Barry's hairs, removed from his head after he was dead, to Samantha Harris. The only reason for the person framing your husband to do that was because that person knew that your husband had left a threatening message on her voice mail system; with that message, and then the envelope turning up, there was just barely enough evidence that your husband might be involved to allow a search warrant to be issued, and of course, the search found Barry's head and hands buried in your backyard. The problem is that not more than another forty yards ahead was a creek, and if someone wanted to dispose of those body parts, they would have walked that little bit further and tossed them in. The creek flows pretty fast; those pieces of Barry would have been miles downstream by the next morning, and there would be no connection to your husband at all. If he'd been the one to try to get rid of them, he would have thought of that."

She looked at him coolly, and Sam realized that he was up against a shrewd woman. "I don't see how that leads you to think I killed Barry."

"Only the killer would have known where Barry's head was, to get the hairs. And the killer would only know to send them to Samantha Harris if she knew that Jimmy had already left an incriminating message on her phone. The only one who knew that, who could possibly have known that, was you, Mrs. Smith."

Mrs. Smith sat there and looked at him calmly. "And how do you intend to prove it, Mr. Prichard?"

Sam shrugged. "Actually, I don't think I need to prove it at all. See, this isn't about me getting your husband out of jail, Mrs. Smith. It's about me taking care of me. I was promised another fifty thousand if I prove he didn't do it. I'd think it would be worth a lot more than that to you for me to forget what I know, don't you?"

She smiled at him. "That depends on how much you want, doesn't it, Mr. Prichard? How much would that be?"

"Your husband told me that he keeps more than half a million here, in cash. I think half of that would make me forget."

Mrs. Smith sat and stared at him for a full minute without saying a word, then smiled again. "And then what? I end up paying you over and over? You keep coming around to collect more when you run out?"

"Nah," Sam said, "I'm not that greedy. With a quarter-million bucks, I can live good in Belize for the rest of my life, and that's what I've got in mind. You only have to pay me once, Mrs. Smith, and I'm out of your hair forever."

She sat there another minute, and Sam was starting to think she wasn't going to go for it. Then she smiled once more.

"Will you wait here, Mr. Prichard, or are you going to insist on going with me to get it?"

"Oh, I'm not letting you out of my sight, Mrs. Smith. Lead the way."

She got up and turned toward the back of the house, and Sam rose to follow. As they walked, he said, "There is one other thing you could do for me, though, just to satisfy my own curiosity."

"And what's that, Mr. Prichard?" she asked.

"Tell me what really happened to Barry. I hate not knowing all the details."

She glanced at him. "And I suppose you're wearing a transmitter? Are the police listening to all of this, Mr. Prichard?"

"God, I hope not, since I just shook you down for a quarter-million dollars! No, I'd seriously just like to know. If you don't want to tell me, that's fine, I was honestly only trying to satisfy my own curiosity."

She smiled but said nothing and walked on into a large room that was decorated like a major corporate office. She went over to a massive chair that sat near a wall, flipped its cushion over and reached down to turn the dial of a safe that was built into its base.

Suddenly she looked up at him. "Barry came over here looking for Jimmy, but he wasn't here. I didn't like Barry very much, not since he was our pool boy for a while back when he was in high school; he always seemed too arrogant for his own good, and I never cared much for him. Anyway, I didn't go to the door when he knocked, I just watched from behind a curtain, and I saw him slip something under a rock outside. That made me wonder what he was up to, so as he was walking away, I stepped out and looked, and it was a note from Samantha Harris, telling Jimmy she wanted to see him again. It said she still loved him, and wanted to talk about getting things going again, and I simply lost my temper."

She looked back down and finished opening the safe, then looked back up at Sam. "I called him, and he turned and saw me and came back. He tried to play innocent with me, and said he was just stopping by to see if Jimmy was home, but I was so mad—I shoved the note in his face and called him liar, and then I just pushed him, and he fell back and hit his head on a rock. He lay there, and I thought, oh, dear God, I've killed him, and I panicked. I decided I needed to get rid of his body. I had some plastic sheeting, and I put that into the bed of Jimmy's old pickup truck, and backed it up close to where he was lying, and then I managed to get him into it. I slammed the tailgate and hid the truck out behind the old woodshed so Jimmy wouldn't see it, and then I got to thinking about where to hide his body. I thought if I cut off his head and his hands it would make it harder to identify him, and something about that got me all excited, so I went and got an ax. I got up in the truck, and swung the ax to chop off one of his hands, and he screamed, and I just about died, but I grabbed the ax and swung it again and hit him in the head with it, and that was it. He was dead, then, so I went ahead and cut off his other hand and then his head. Do you know, Mr. Prichard, that it took me five chops to get his head off?"

Sam stood there, staring at her as she described murder and dismemberment, and barely managed to answer. "Yeah," he said. "Those neck bones can be pretty tough."

"Anyway, I put those parts in a big plastic trash bag and hid them in the woodshed, then waited 'til way past midnight and drove the truck out by the Air Force Base and rolled him out of it. I didn't come up with the idea to hang it on Jimmy 'til the next day, when I heard him calling that tramp and telling her to stay out of it. That made me madder, and I knew that if she got some parts of Barry, she'd go to the cops, and with that message, I figured they'd come search our place, so I cut off a piece of his scalp and mailed it to her, then took the bag with the head and stuff, and buried it out there that afternoon. Then it was just a waiting game."

"Why did you agree to let him hire me?"

She shrugged, as if to say she didn't know if it was going to rain or not. "I didn't think there was any way you'd figure out it was me. I thought I'd covered my tracks too well for that, so I figured, sure, let him have a little hope. It'd make me look all that much more innocent, the poor wife, all worried about hubby, right? Seemed like a good idea at the time. Now it's gonna cost me another quarter million, but I've got everything else, and he'll still be gone. Works for me. The bastard should never have played around with those whores of his!"

She looked down at the open safe, and then reached in and took out a bag and began filling it with stacks of money. "Would you come over here for a moment, Mr. Prichard?" Sam walked slowly over to where she was standing, and she pointed into the safe. "As you can see, Mr. Prichard, I am giving you exactly what you asked for, two hundred and fifty thousand dollars in cash. I'm not even deducting the fifty thousand you already got from me, but what I really wanted you to see, Mr. Prichard, is the pistol that was lying in the top of the safe. I could easily have pulled it out and shot you just now, Mr. Prichard, while you were so engrossed in my story, but I didn't. I find that I can't sleep very well since I killed Barry; he haunts me, even in the daytime. I keep seeing him everywhere I go, everywhere I look, so I didn't want to kill you, Mr. Prichard. I don't need another ghost to haunt me."

She closed the bag and offered it to Sam, but he didn't take it. Instead, he said, "I don't want your money, Mrs. Smith. All I wanted was to get you to confess to murder, and you just did. You asked if I was wearing a transmitter, and I said no, because I'm not. You don't need one, not in the age of cell phones. All I did was call Detective Parks and told her where I was going and that I was going to ask you to pay me off to keep me quiet, and that all she needed to do was listen in, because I left the line wide open." He took his phone out of his shirt pocket, and showed her the red light that said it was in an active call and on speakerphone setting. "Did you get it all, Karen?"

A tiny voice came from the phone. "Every word, Sam, and all of it recorded. We're driving into the estate now."

Sam put the phone back into his pocket, took the bag of money from her hand and set it back down in the safe, then closed it. He took Sheila Smith by her arm and walked her out through the house and into the waiting arms of Detective Karen Parks of the Denver Police Department's Homicide Division.

"You're coming down to give a statement, aren't you, Sam?" Karen asked.

"Yeah," he said, "I'll be there shortly. I need to go see my client first, is that okay? I think I should be the one to tell him."

She nodded. "That's fine, I want to see you right after, though. And I'll see that he's released when you get there."

Sam nodded, and walked over to get into his van. He drove back to the jail, and the jailer smiled when he walked in.

"I got a phone call from the prosecutor's office a little while ago, and they said to release Mr. Smith to you, Mr. Prichard. He's almost through processing, and will be right up."

Sam just nodded. "Don't tell him anything yet," he said. "I think I should be the one to tell him what's going on."

"No problem, all we know is that the charge against him has been dismissed, and we're to let you take him out of here. He should be done in just a few minutes."

Sam sat down in a chair and waited, and about ten minutes later, Jimmy Smith was escorted out of the jail. He saw Sam and broke into a huge grin.

"Sam! You did it, man, you did it! I don't know how to thank you!" He reached out and grabbed Sam's hand, and shook it 'til Sam thought it was going to come off.

Sam finally got it back. "Look, Jimmy," he said as they walked out the door into the sunlight, "there's something I gotta tell you..."

"Well, first, just tell me who it was who did this to me! That's what I want to know more than anything!"

Sam nodded. "Well, that's part of it. I did find out who really killed Barry, and who was trying to frame you for it, but I don't think you're gonna be all that glad." He cleared his throat. "Jimmy—it was your wife, Sheila. She caught Barry bringing you a note from Samantha Harris, and lost her mind over it, and she hit him and thought she'd killed him, so she was trying to hide his body before you found it."

Smith looked shocked, his eyes wide and his mouth open. He tried to say something twice, and then managed to croak out, "Sheila..."

"Yeah. She had it in her head that if she cut off his hands and his head, it'd make it harder to identify him, so she got an ax and chopped off a hand, but he wasn't dead, and he screamed, and—well, then she hit him in the head with the ax, and that pretty much did him in. She went ahead and cut his other hand and his head off, and then dumped the body that night out where it was found. I don't know where she kept his head and hands, but she planted them in the yard and sent the hairs off to Samantha to get back at you for your affairs."

Smith was just staring out through the windshield as Sam drove, and didn't say anything more for a long time. Sam brought him along to the police department so that he could talk to the detective, and gave his statement to another cop while Karen talked to Smith. When he was done, he drove Smith to his house.

He parked in the driveway and let Smith out, then started to drive away.

"Hey!" Smith yelled at him. "Aren't you forgetting something?"

Sam stopped and looked at him. "What?"

Jimmy managed a weak smile. "Hell, man, I owe you another fifty thousand dollars! Aren't you gonna come and get it?"

Sam looked at him. "Mail me a check," he said, and drove out of the estate. He had one more stop to make before he considered himself finished, and wanted to get it over with.

He rang the doorbell and waited only a moment before Samantha Harris answered. "Mr. Prichard," she said, seeming surprised to see him. "What can I do for you?"

"You can answer just one question for me, Miss Harris, and then I'll go and leave you alone. You told me that it was Barry who called Jimmy Smith from your phone, and when I told you that Jimmy said it was you, you insisted that it was Barry. Trouble is, I'm quite certain now that you lied about that, and to be perfectly honest, I just need to know why. It was you who called Jimmy, wasn't it? Tell me why you lied to me."

She looked for a moment like she was going to get angry, but then she seemed to collapse into herself. She looked at him for a long moment, and then said, "Barry died at Jimmy's place, didn't he?"

Sam nodded. "He did," he said, "but it wasn't Jimmy who killed him. It was his wife, Sheila. She killed him because she said she caught him bringing Jimmy a note from you, saying that you wanted to start up your affair again."

The woman almost did collapse, then, and had to lean against the doorframe for support. "Oh, my God," she said. "Oh, God, I didn't know—I asked Barry to take the note because he said he was going to go and tell Jimmy in person that he wasn't going to sign. I never dreamed he'd run into her..."

"But he did, and now he's dead. Why did you really call Jimmy that day?"

She sighed. "I did call to tell him Barry wouldn't sign," she said, "but I was gonna tell him I thought I could talk him into it. He never gave me a chance, though; he started yelling at me and saying I was the reason Barry wasn't listening to him. The truth was, I thought if I got Barry to sign, he might take me back, and maybe he'd realize how good we were together."

"So you sent Barry there to leave a note saying you loved him? That's all it was? And you thought you could get Barry to go ahead and leave the band, so you were trying to use that to get close to Jimmy again?" He shook his head. "You didn't mean for anything bad to happen, I get that—but in the long run, it was your selfishness that cost Barry his life, and took away the future he could have had. You're an amazing piece of work, Miss Harris."

Sam turned and walked away, ignoring the weeping woman who was shouting that she was sorry.

He got home about three in the afternoon, and told Indie all of it. She was as shocked as he had been at the way it had all turned out, but she went with him to Stan's garage to meet up with the band. They were all there, fresh from Barry's funeral, just waiting after Sam had called them and asked them to get together, and he sat in one of the folding chairs and told the whole story again.

Chris stared into space, Stan got angry and began to

pace around, Candy just sat there, and Janice went and sat in the grass outside and cried. Indie went and sat with her for a while, and finally the two of them came back into the garage.

"At least we know what happened," Janice said, "and that means a lot, Sam."

"Yeah, man, it does," Chris said.

They sat and talked a little longer, and then Sam said he wasn't up to rehearsing that evening, so he and Indie went home to be with Kenzie.

They sat in the dining room and played Go Fish and Old Maid with her for a little while, but Kenzie was more interested in playing with Samson, so they let her go. Sam and Indie gathered up all the papers she'd printed out on the case and put them into a file, and marked it "Closed," then went to make dinner. No one was feeling very energetic, so they settled for tuna salad sandwiches and chips that night.

They decided to watch a movie, and Sam said he wanted to see a comedy. He said life was too much sometimes, and he just needed a good laugh or two, so they found a movie that sounded good, and laughed themselves silly. By the time it was over, it was time for Kenzie to go to bed, and Sam and Indie went to bed only a few minutes later.

Sam was too quiet, Indie said, so she put some effort into getting his attention, and a few minutes later it dawned on him that everything was alright in his world.

The sun came through the curtains, which had been opened, and woke Sam around eight the next morning. He rolled over and saw that Indie wasn't there, so he got up and showered and went out to the kitchen. She was making omelets, and Kenzie was at the table. Sam put his finger to his lips, and Kenzie smiled and did the same as he snuck up on Indie and grabbed her from behind, then began kissing her neck and ears.

She squealed. "Sam!" she said. "Darn it, I've *told* you what that does to me! Stop it, or I'll sleep upstairs tonight!"

"Fine, fine," he said, but he let her go and went to sit at the table with Kenzie. A few minutes later they were all eating omelets, and laughing and talking normally once again.

"So," Sam said, "today we are going car shopping, but I was thinking that I already have one car too many, so I thought we'd trade off the van, and get us a family vehicle. I can drive the Vette as my personal car, and if I need the bigger car, you can drive it."

Indie looked at him. "Um, Sam—I can't drive a stick shift."

Sam smiled at her. "You can learn," he said. "I'll teach you, and soon you'll be begging to drive the Vette! We'll just buy an extra car seat for Kenzie and keep it in the garage, for when one of us needs to take her somewhere in it."

Indie smiled, and seemed excited about learning to

drive the Corvette, but she was more interested in what kind of car they were going to buy that day.

"I don't know," Sam said. "An SUV, maybe, something with four-wheel drive, for the snow in the winter?"

"Now, that might be a good idea," Indie said. "I hate driving in the wintertime, but four-wheel drive would make it a lot better."

"And an SUV would mean more room for grocery shopping and such. I think we're onto something, here. Let's all get dressed and ready, and we'll go."

Kenzie ran up the stairs, with Indie yelling at her not to run up the stairs. Indie went to change out of her nightgown, and Sam followed her and watched, his eyes roaming over her body as he smiled.

She caught him looking. "What?" she asked with a grin.

He smiled at her. "Baby," he said, "I'm just admiring the view!"

BOOK 3
LOVE AND WAR

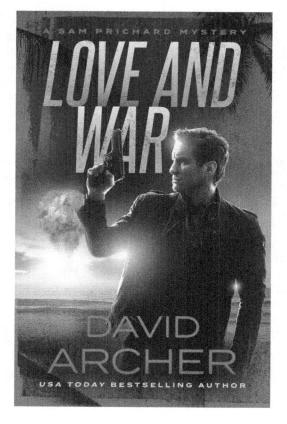

AVAILABLE ON AMAZON

ABOUT

David Archer was born and raised in Bakersfield, California. He is a fiction author and novelist, writing in the mysteries and thrillers genre. His approach to writing is to hit deep, keep you entertained, and leave you wanting MORE with every turn of the page. He writes mysteries, thrillers, and suspense novels, all of which are primed to get your heart pumping.

The author's books are a mixture of mystery, action, suspense, and humor. If you're looking for a good place to start, take a look at his bestselling Sam Prichard Novels, available now. You can grab copies in eBook, Audio, or Paperback on all major retailers.

Made in the USA
Coppell, TX
05 August 2020